THE KILBOURNE CONNECTION

Gaylord D. Larsen

THE KILBOURNE CONNECTION

Bethany Fellowship INC.
MINNEAPOLIS, MINNESOTA 55438

To Vic and Della
In Memory

The Kilbourne Connection
Gaylord D. Larsen

Library of Congress Catalog Card Number 80-67904

ISBN 0-87123-305-3

Published by Bethany Fellowship, Inc.
6820 Auto Club Road, Minneapolis, Minnesota 55438

Printed in the United States of America

About the Author

Gaylord Larsen is a media specialist at Ventura Community College in California, where he develops instructional materials for instructors, and also teaches. He has been a freelance writer, a religious film producer, a network representative for Young and Rubicam Advertising, an instructor for Los Angeles Community College District, and a film editor for ABC-TV, Hollywood. He is a member of the Writer's Guild of America-West, and a member of Ventura Community Presbyterian Church. He is married and the father of four children.

Thursday

Henry had been a great believer in premonitions, but when the phone rang he was in the garden thinking only of his hibiscus bushes and wondering why they weren't blooming.

His wife rapped on the living room window, "It's for you, dear."

"Who is it?" he called without rising from his gentleman farmer's squat. Three months earlier he would have hurried into the house, but no more; he had noticed lately that even his mind was operating more slowly now. So much had changed in his life. Why, he didn't know.

The woman at the window shrugged and turned away. It was her way of saying, "You know you will have to come in and answer it anyway."

Henry rose, wincing at the familiar hitch in his 52-year-old back; he waddled along the freeform stone path, finally reaching his full height as he opened the back door.

"This is Mr. Garrott."

"Henry? Is this Henry Garrott?"

"Yes."

"You ol' son-of-a-gun. How are you? Had a heck of a time locating you. When did you move to California?"

"Who *is* this?"

"Vern McCarthy. Remember—you did a job for us in Belgium? I was with the State Department."

"Oh, yes . . . well, I'm out of government service."

"So am I, Henry," McCarthy said ebulliently. "I'm with the Kilbourne Group just up the coast from you in Marbol County."

"Oh, yes," Henry answered dryly.

"I'm one of the directors. You must have read about it. It was in all the eastern papers."

"I guess I missed it," Henry said, squinting as he tried to

visualize the man on the other end of the line.

Then he remembered a short, plump man with thinning sandy hair, sitting in a little foreign restaurant someplace, his thick glasses tipped up at an angle trying to read a smudged menu. His voice was his dominant feature—always bubbling, expectant, enthusiastic. He ordered a glass of buttermilk so eagerly, Henry recalled, that he almost joined him in spite of his natural loathing for the drink. Vern McCarthy was the perfect escort and aid for frustrated American tourists, but Henry couldn't see him advancing very high in the Department. That sense of euphoria his voice generated had to wear a bit thin after a time, especially among the cool heads at the helm of any foreign embassy. He had probably been "invited" out.

The Kilbourne Group would be a logical move. It would be a nice boost in pay. The State Department would have given him a prestigious title for a year with the understanding that he move on. The Kilbourne Group, although now a privately endowed think-tank, still needed lucrative government grants, and there was no better way to nurture necessary contacts than to hire a highly recommended "fireball" from the State Department for their Board of Directors.

The speed with which these thoughts crackled through Henry's mind amazed him. He may have missed a word or two about Vern McCarthy's move west, but it was all clicking inside just as before. Without one piece of hard evidence, he had assembled the whole stream of events in mid-conversation— and he could stake his life upon the validity of ninety percent of it. Old habits die hard.

"Listen, Henry, the reason I'm calling is, we have a bit of a problem here that would be right up your alley."

"What's that?"

"Well, it's one of those things I don't want to get into over the phone. I think it would be about a week's, maybe ten days', work at the most for you. You could do everything right here at the Center and in town."

"And you're not going to tell me what it entails?"

"Henry, please . . . it'll pay well. I'll work it out so it looks like you're a special consultant. Well, you *are* actually."

"Vernon, to tell the truth, it doesn't sound as if I'm your man."

"Why not?"

"Because I've become a Christian."

"What's that?" Vern's buoyant voice suddenly struck like an axe.

"I've become a Christian." Henry could feel his cheeks heating up; why did he get into this anyway? "It means I've accepted Jesus Christ as my—"

"I know what it means. What has that got to do with anything?"

"Well, I'm still sorting things out and I don't do—won't operate the way we did sometimes."

"Listen, you misunderstand, Henry. This is strictly a simple—I swear it's right up your alley. No problems."

"And I'm scheduled to meet with an accounting firm here in town regarding a position."

"Can't you put it off a week? Listen, old boy, we need your expertise."

Henry wondered what "expertise" he possessed that was so valuable to McCarthy. Silence?

They began repeating themselves, then finally agreeing that Henry would call back that evening with a decision after talking with his wife and the prospective employer.

One thing puzzled Henry about the matter: There was no secret regarding his whereabouts; why hadn't McCarthy gotten in touch with his former bureau in Washington for Henry's address?

"Sorry I didn't get the chap's name before," Valery apologized.

Henry was still sitting with his hand on the phone when his wife entered the living room. "Oh, no problem," he said blankly.

"Anything important?" she asked.

They had evolved this family ritual of her asking about his work and Henry always putting her off with generalities. The necessity for this was understood by both parties, but the ritual endured for the sake of light conversation. But now that their youngest child was in college and with Henry no longer involved with security matters, he had resolved to be more open with her. Valery relieved the piano fern of some dying sprigs;

then with a bemused expression she came to sit opposite her husband as he told her of the curious request McCarthy had made.

"Do you want to do it?" Valery asked.

"What about the bedroom?"

"We'll simply have to wait and wallpaper it after the new furniture arrives."

"Can you handle the delivery people alone?"

She laughed. "Henry, of the dozens of moves we've made, I can't remember one time when you were on hand to help."

She wanted him to go, that was obvious. There was nothing pressing that couldn't be delayed a week; this would be a good opportunity to test his own confidence and he wondered at himself for hesitating.

He watched his wife's hands as she neatly organized the wilted pieces of fern she would soon throw away. She looked as he had seen her a thousand times before, wearing two matching sweaters and a tweed skirt and surrounded by the heavy old pieces of furniture they had mostly inherited from her parents. Now in their 'new' old English Tudor house, she looked very much at home.

"It's been a tough life for you, hasn't it?"

"Me? Absolutely not." She smiled and waited but he said nothing.

"Of course, it's up to you." She rose and started to leave the room, then came back behind the couch and kissed his cheek. "We'll start wallpapering in the morning if you like."

Henry watched her go and marveled at what a great writer Henry James was.

Without saying a word about the *matter*, Valery had expressed herself eloquently and lovingly in Jamesian understatement. It had not been her custom to give Henry casual pecks on the cheek or to table an issue quite so quickly. But that unspoken inflection in her voice, or the kiss, or her leaving the room at the precise moment she did, without waiting for an answer he wasn't ready to give, assured him, "I'm with you. I don't understand it all, but I love you."

Henry, at first, had been deeply hurt because of her part in his recent "incarceration," but time and a better understanding of Valery's point of view had changed his feelings some-what. It was still there between them; perhaps more on Valery's consciousness than his own, but it still colored both their thoughts.

Henry had brought it on himself in a way. Or perhaps more accurately, circumstances which Henry did not choose to alter had brought it about.

Henry never felt he possessed the temperament for CIA work, but a series of flukes led him into it. During the Korean conflict, he had not hesitated to grab the chance for transfer to the intelligence-gathering arm of the Signal Corps. His infantry division had been scheduled to embark within the week for what they knew would be front-line duty, when his orders were changed. Years later, he discovered that the old cavalry general responsible for selecting him had been an avid reader of westerns—Henry had been singled out because he had a college degree, and because his last name resembled that of an old western hero the general had taken a liking to.

His college training in accounting served him well. Henry developed a knack for building projections on the North Korean's activities, solely on the basis of their expenditures for food rations. He constantly analyzed smuggled supply lists and civilian reports, and when one regiment was found to be fed better than others, it was invariably because of a military goal.

Henry's success continued when he was transferred to counter-intelligence in the European sectors. The heavy-handed Russian system left obvious signs of what they were up to if one only knew how to read them. Suspected spies were never hard to spot. The difficult task was discerning who was doing what. That's where Henry's team came in.

The more important a spy's work was to the Russians, the better the spy lived. Not only bank accounts, but taxi rides, pressed suits, even cuff links and rich desserts—or no desserts—helped to identify these mysterious people's stations on the pecking orders and cross-filed indexes, which led to more revelations. Soon the secrets vanished and it became a game—a game the Russians never became skilled at playing, at least not until Henry moved on.

It was during this time that Henry, like the others in his group, began to view people as stereotypes—third echelon Czechs and silly little hofbraus with husbands in Russia. The stereotypes became objects to be manipulated—all for a good cause, of course.

Then, as often happens in organizations of any size, Henry was promoted out of his area of expertise into one of incompetence. Diplomatic espionage and intrigue were not the forte of this introspective, quiet man, but he muddled through as best he could.

Different events and scenes of his career kept popping into Henry's mind now, and because he had time, he would run them over and over like an old movie, searching for things he might have done differently, or to gain some new perspective of himself.

He thrust his hands into his pockets and ambled out into his garden. The beauty of the garden had been one big reason they had purchased the California house. The former owners were professional florists and had developed their brick-walled backyard to perfection. But Henry's amateur enthusiasm for gardening, he was discovering, was not enough to keep things growing properly. His own laziness and inexperience with Southern California climate and plants were beginning to show. His front lawn was already losing color from being watered in the heat of the day.

As he picked up a trowel, his mind whirled back to another garden in the Hague. A businessman he had met at the embassy had invited him over to see his spring garden during a small gathering of horticulturalists. But among the rather elite group of guests had been a German couple the British suspected of passing secret data to the East Germans.

The wife, a beautiful woman perhaps 15 years younger than her husband, had had access to classified NATO documents by virtue of her secretarial position. Henry had been startled when he had glanced through the foliage of a swan-shaped shrub and spotted the couple in the far corner of the garden. He had scrutinized them for nearly a full minute, intent on . . . on what?

He tried to picture in his mind, again, what it was about the couple that had mesmerized him. He knew from his first glance there was no love between them. It was something else. The wife was nervous and imploring, without real animation. But the husband's queer expression, staring only at the plants, troubled Henry. He was the one who should be investigated.

But Henry did nothing about it. Five days later, the husband was in East Germany, and two days after, one of the CIA's important spy networks was annihilated; and two of Henry's close friends were dead.

Henry then began to doubt his own worth, and the worth of all their efforts. From the secretary-wife they learned all they needed to know—all that Henry's intuition had already told him. The marriage had never been consummated. The husband had married the girl to gain entry to the right circles. The day of the garden party was the first time the wife knew of his activities and was in the process of confronting him when Henry spotted them. Henry told himself a thousand times that, for all he really knew, they could have been arguing about who left the cap off the toothpaste.

But it was no good. It was his job to be suspicious, and he had fumbled the ball.

It would have been a simple matter—just a word to a co-worker in another office, and the husband could have been detained and investigated. Instead, the issue had been put out of mind. He had not forgotten or discounted what he felt in his gut about the couple. But why had he not acted? Why? Why?

Back in his own garden he looked up toward the living room window in time to see his wife disappear. He caught an expression of deep concern on her face, and it was only then he realized he was wearing a heavy scowl and had been jabbing the trowel aimlessly into a box of compost.

There was no getting around it now; he'd have to go up and see what McCarthy wanted. He wasn't resolving anything sitting around the house regretting the past; and he was driving his wife bananas. Henry started scattering the compost around the base of some plants and prayed, "Lord, I hope what Paul told Timothy is true, 'For God has not given us the spirit of fear, but of power, and of love, and of a sound mind.'"

Friday

Early the next morning, Valery had his large brown suitcase packed and waiting for him at the front door. Her father, a career man in the Department of Commerce, had been stationed in England during much of Valery's youth, and a servant always placed her father's valise at the front door in such a manner when he traveled. Henry had asked her many times not to bother, but to no avail. In many ways she was more British than the British. She had also strapped his large grey umbrella neatly on the side of the suitcase in her usual manner; and rather than lecture her again on the probability of a June rain in Southern California, he decided to take it along.

En route to the train depot they made tentative plans for Valery to drive up later the next week, if his work assignment went well, and they would drive on up the California coast, which neither of them had seen.

They exchanged their usual discreet good-byes at the train; Henry boarded and seated himself by a window on the ocean side. Glancing out the window, he noticed Valery still standing on the platform gazing at him. The train gave no indication of moving, so he decided to walk to the loading door and chat.

He no sooner got there than the train started groaning forward.

"Good-bye, darling, I love you!" he called to her with his best reassuring smile.

"Henry, I'm sorry—" She walked a few steps, stopped and waved him out of sight.

Henry plopped contentedly back into his seat and watched the scenery begin racing by; he felt better than he had in weeks. In his mind he again savored his wife's call, "Henry, I'm sorry—" After twenty-three years of marriage!

His move from Europe back to Washington was ostensibly a routine transfer; however, it was designed to satisfy two of the agency's needs. Henry's effectiveness in its European operations had dwindled. More importantly, the Washington office was being quietly investigated by an unsympathetic congressional committee. Henry was granted a title comparable to chargé d'affaires, so he would be the primary congressional contact; since he knew little of the Washington operations, he could honestly avoid giving any embarrassing answers to committee investigators. Meanwhile, all the knowledgeable agents had suddenly received important assignments in various parts of the globe. It was one more game in a series of games that had begun to gnaw at Henry, and he was a ripe candidate for change.

Then last fall the change came, initiated from an unexpected source; Henry had struck up a friendly relationship with a young Congressman from Iowa—a member of the committee Henry was supposed to be showing around. The friendliness, at first, was all on the Congressman's part, for he had a habit of asking personal questions that disconcerted Henry. Since his adulthood, he couldn't recall any casual acquaintance vitally interested in his personal activities, so he held the Congressman at a distance while searching for his hidden motives. No one, he thought, beams a smile at another human being just from the sheer joy of communing with a fellow creature.

The motive surfaced when Henry was invited to a Bible study and prayer group sponsored by a group of Christians on the Hill. In order to garner a few brownie points with the investigators, he had made his initial visit. Then a second and third visit, and by winter, he found it was part of his weekly routine.

The attraction at first was the open, warm fellowship of the men; yes, even the somehow slightly obscene sight of plump middle-aged government leaders in pinstriped suits embracing one another. The willingness of powerful people to bare their weaknesses and shortcomings to others in the group, without fear of political retribution, also appealed to him.

Later on, it was the message preached—the same message his Aunt Mildred made him go to Sunday school to hear, only now it seemed different. Now it seemed cloaked in a positive realism an adult could consider substantive.

The thought of Aunt Mildred led Henry's mind onto one more detour. After twenty-five years of ignoring her memory, he found she was in his consciousness again, and it was usually the same indelible scene.

Henry had been a sophomore or junior in high school when his father had made him go along to visit her in the hospital. She had always fussed over Henry, perhaps as the child she never had; and Henry's father, though never kind to his sister in happy times, had become very conciliatory during her illness, and wanted the boy along to cheer her.

Henry, not realizing the gravity of her illness, wearily slouched in a corner of the room, reading the Sunday funnies, while his dad sat in the other corner with the Sports section, glacing occasionally at his sleeping sister. His father muttered something about leaving, when Henry looked up from "Prince Valiant" to see his aunt's eyes gazing blankly at him; then her stare rolled over to the ceiling above her brother's head and there was a flush of recognition. Her face became animated as though meeting an old friend. She thrust her arms toward the corner of the room and joyfully reached out farther and farther—and tumbled headfirst onto the cold terrazzo floor.

Pandemonium ensued as Henry's father rushed about, swearing and yelling for help; then he and the nurses tucked the patient back into bed, straightened her hair and bed clothes, and looked after the broken collarbone. All through this Henry stood transfixed, afraid of the problems of the elderly and mortified at seeing his aunt's bare, thin white legs flopping about in plain view. In spite of all their busyness, it was several minutes before they discovered Aunt Mildred was dead.

Somehow, in Henry's young mind, evangelical Christianity had become inexorably linked with Aunt Mildred's fragile white legs and the deaths of old-fashioned people. But with the advancing years, and the specter of his own death rising before him, Henry had become more interested in the other aspect of this traumatic scene: *What had his aunt been reaching for in her last moment on earth?*

The leap of faith required to embrace life-changing, born-again Christianity became increasingly attractive to Henry. He was introduced to the writings of C. S. Lewis and Richard Halverson. He was enthralled with the love and support he found with his new friends. He was impressed with the authority of the rediscovered New Testament. And finally, he was persuaded. One spring morning, riding the subway between the Capitol and the House Office Building with his Congressman friend from Iowa, he quietly committed his life to Christ.

The emotional lift he experienced no doubt contributed to his subsequent slip in judgment. That noon, at a luncheon with some twenty of his co-workers and two Congressmen with their aides, he decided to publicly declare what had transpired in his life. He started to tell of finding a personal relationship with the God of the universe who loved and cared for him as an individual, but as he spoke, the amazing significance of the concept struck him for the first time. Great tears welled up in his eyes and ran down his cheeks, and he could not go on. Sitting now in a train, thousands of miles away from the event, Henry grinned at his own embarrassment. Remembering the stony looks of disbelief from his co-workers, Henry laughed out loud and the heads of two little girls in the seat ahead of him popped up to see what was so funny.

But there had been nothing funny about it at the time. In fact, it was deadly serious, for such deportment in a public meeting could mean only one thing. Before Henry knew what was happening, he was discreetly cajoled and elbowed into a locked ward of what turned out to be a mental hospital for Washington VIPs. The Central Intelligence Agency, employed by the government dedicated to religious and civil freedom, knew a crackpot when it saw one. His wife was informed and persuaded to sign temporary commitment papers.

Poor Valery. She was quite religious herself, in her own way. Her idea of Christianity was keeping the trains running on time, speaking kindly with proper English to those less fortunate, and extending a certain amount of charity through the right channels. The notion of a personal emotional link with Deity was completely foreign to her. Obviously her husband needed help.

Ten days passed before his Congressman friend could arrange Henry's release, and it was a very shaky Christian convert who emerged. Perhaps, as his psychiatrist had suggested, Henry could no longer face the stresses of his real world and was using religion as a means of escape. Perhaps, as the agency people implied, religion was not discussed by intelligent people.

Henry soon realized he was no longer considered stable enough to handle sensitive security matters, and when the generous retirement arrangement was offered he accepted. His debriefing was minimal; he was given a look at a list of activities that were never to be discussed, a phone number and address to contact in an emergency, and that was all. Nothing was said about the three large Swiss bank accounts in Henry's name, funds which could be released only with Henry's signature. "Sloppy work," Henry thought, and allowed himself the luxury of sighing, "Not like the good old days."

The large depot sign announcing "Almaden Village" rolled into view as the train rumbled slowly to a halt. Henry fumbled about for his belongings and realized he had just ridden seventy-three miles and couldn't recall one bit of scenery along the way.

There was no sign of McCarthy at the platform or at the parking lot fronting the small depot. Henry was about to wave a taxi over when he heard the horn of a Mercedes in the third row over, and spotted Vern McCarthy's arm gyrating to get his attention.

"Glad you could make it. Very glad." McCarthy gave Henry a quick handshake, tossed Henry's gear into the back seat of the 450 SEL, and they sped off. After a brief lecture on the importance of having one's own car in California, McCarthy fell silent. The car droned effortlessly along a winding, old concrete road which hugged the foothills. Shortly, they began climbing, the turns became sharper, and the houses along the road newer.

Almaden was originally a fishing village on the narrow strip of flat land pinched between the steep foothills and the ocean. As the fishing declined, artists and poets moved in, and cantilevered A-frames began dotting the treacherous hillsides.

The Mercedes pulled off on a graveled shoulder designed for sightseers. McCarthy said, "C'mon," and hopped out of the car and walked to an observation bench some fifty feet away. Henry tagged along, deciding to let McCarthy get to the point in his own sweet time.

The midmorning sun gave the smooth, blue-grey Pacific a texture so solid one could be tempted to skateboard all the way to Hawaii.

"That's our center over there." McCarthy gestured toward an adjoining hillside. To Henry, surveying the low, sprawling building complex, it looked more like a retaining wall than the home of genius.

"Very impressive," Henry replied.

McCarthy became fidgety. He picked up some loose stones as if to cascade them down the empty ravine before them, but thought better of it and dropped them.

"We're in trouble," he began, "big financial trouble."

"What do you mean? According to *Fortune* magazine, you're the most heavily endowed think-tank—"

"That *Fortune* article is two years old." McCarthy interrupted with an edge on his voice, then smiled self-consciously as though he'd exposed too much. "A lot of those endowments had strings attached. You ever heard of A. K. Shoemaker?"

"Mmmm . . . he was on the President's Commission on Education a few years back. That who you mean?"

McCarthy nodded slowly. "He did the groundwork for the Head Start Program—you know, preschoolers. He came here to the group with a lot of hoopla, as I hear it. He's got a free ride. A full fellowship at $53,000 a year, with plenty of research money. And he gets into this genetic study and publishes these blasted papers—"

"What genetic study?"

"He's come up with this theory about blacks and intelligence quotients. The more dark pigmentation in the gene, the lower the I.Q. potential."

"Oh, yes, I guess I did read—"

"The man just won't leave it alone. Every time he goes on a talk show, he carries the Kilbourne name with him, and our prestige goes," he gestured down the ravine. "The Ford Foundation has pulled out and the Lippmann people are looking for legal holes to free their commitments—the NAACP is after them.

"The irony of the whole thing is, Shoemaker's monies are from a science endowment, and are unaffected, but *we're* getting it in the neck."

"Too bad," Henry consoled, "but he's just one man. Surely he can't destroy the prestige of an organization like this."

McCarthy shook his head. "Eighty-five percent of our non-government funding was from politically liberal sources. Liberalism isn't the popular cause it once was, and all they need is an excuse like this—"

McCarthy was interrupted by the sound of an old station wagon pulling off the road near them. Two mothers unloaded an army of children for sight-seeing. Screeching and miscellaneous picnic clamor ensued. An irritated McCarthy watched them, and Henry watched McCarthy. Why was he so jumpy? His voice and mannerisms were not at all as Henry remembered. Why were they having this conversation out here away from the car? Could it be bugged?

"I can see you have a problem, but I don't see how I can help," Henry said.

"Let me finish," McCarthy said and moved around so his back was to the sightseers. "We've had to dip very heavily into the general fund to meet expenses, and last Monday I got a call from our bank. Our balance is thirty-seven hundred dollars." He punched the sum out as if there were a monumental significance to it.

"So?"

"Good grief, man, there's supposed to be over a million dollars in that account!" He was on tiptoes.

"Calm down," Henry said. He couldn't look at McCarthy just then, so he stretched his legs by walking over to the guard rail, then back, finally sitting down on the bench.

"You mean to say your group has maintained a regular checking account with a million-dollar balance?"

"Listen, this was started long before I came on the scene."

"Who's your accountant?"

"You've got to understand how the center works. Every

person with a full fellowship chair is given a full vote on the administrative council. Sabbatical-leave professors each have a third of a vote."

"I get the picture."

"General Kilbourne set it up that way to avoid some of the politics the groups back east—"

"And they hired you as a director?"

"Director-in-residence, which means administrator. The other five are just figureheads who meet twice a year."

"I need to know who works with your accountant or treasurer."

The life drained out of McCarthy's face. "We don't have one," he answered lamely.

Henry blinked. "Do you understand what I'm asking? The books . . . who does—"

"Two years ago when money started getting tight, Mr. MacKenzie retired. He was a close friend of General Kilbourne I'm told, and managed all finances. He really controlled things. Anyway, he apparently was resented by several group members, and with him out of the way, they weren't about to turn such power over to someone else. They decided not to fill the Comptroller position, in spite of the governing rules' stipulation. They've been taking turns keeping the books."

"I see," Henry said, slipping off his coat and draping it over his knee.

"All this was started before my time," McCarthy repeated. He seemed to be quieting down now, perhaps relieved to be sharing his burden with someone else.

"How do you know there is a million dollars missing?"

"Because when I came on board eight months ago, I asked for a general accounting. I don't know much about finances, but I did know enough to ask—"

"Did you get that information from the books," Henry interrupted, "or from the bank balance?"

"From the bank balance. I couldn't make head nor tail out of the books. We had one million four hundred, and some thousand in the account then. I've tried to tally up all the expenses that would have been paid out of that account and the total has got to be well over a million." He said it with a strong emphasis as if the conviction of his voice would be enough to make it so.

"Who's handling the books now?"

"When I came on board it was Dr. Peterson; in March he turned it over to Dr. Begelman."

"Fyodor Begelman?" Henry asked with a surprised smile. "The Nobel Prize winner?"

"Yes."

Henry rose and swung his coat over his shoulder, kicking some loose gravel about as he walked in a circle around their bench. He was still smiling, shaking his head.

"Do you know him?" McCarthy asked.

"I never met the man," Henry said. "It just strikes me funny—the thought of a great mind like that doing the books. Are janitorial supplies in that account?"

"If you think that's funny, you're going to have a hilarious time here."

"You know," Henry crossed his arms and looked out to sea, "it's been my experience, if you take an expert out of his field of concentration, he's something of an innocent."

"I'll drink to that." McCarthy groaned with a trace of bitterness that didn't escape Henry.

"These aren't the kind of people that embezzle funds. There's got to be some simple, logical explanation to this. Some mistake . . . " Henry looked to McCarthy for a sign of agreement but none came. "Don't you agree?"

"That's what *you're* here to find out," McCarthy said with a shrug.

Henry wiped the perspiration off the back of his neck with his handkerchief. McCarthy, with his open polo shirt and light-colored shoes and slacks, seemed impervious to the baking sun.

"Shall we go?" Henry asked.

"One more thing," McCarthy demanded, rising but not moving. "We can't put up with any more bad press, so I'm hoping you can look into this on the Q.T."

"That's going to be a bit difficult."

"Why so?" McCarthy asked.

"I may be able to solve your problem by just checking

check stubs, and so on, but more than likely, I'll have to interview people that had access—"

"Now listen, let me give you the background."

Henry smiled to himself at the old State Department jargon; invariably, "getting the background" meant "looking at the problem from my point of view."

Vern McCarthy launched into his many reasons for secrecy: the group was on the verge of important discoveries in the genetic field, there was a big federal grant for birth control study in the wings, much of the success of a think-tank depended upon its high standards and pure research. Once it lost that image, it was doomed.

"I don't care about the money. I just want to hold things together till this government grant hits—scrape up enough to pay the bills and stop the leak. If this comes out now, as if somebody stole the money, everything will unravel and I'll be out in the . . . " He rubbed the back of his right hand.

" . . . cold." Henry finished for him, and caught himself smiling again. Why did he keep doing that? He never did that on the job before. If anything, he had always been too serious.

"I know I got this job on a lark," McCarthy continued, "and maybe some people think I'm in over my head; maybe some people want me to fail." He stepped close to Henry, too close for the great outdoors. "But I'm not going to fail. You're going to help me, and I'm not going to fail."

"Yes . . . well." Henry shifted his coat from one shoulder to the other to create a little breathing room. Henry was considerably taller than McCarthy, and he knew they had to look a bit weird, jammed together that way.

"Now let's work out something to tell the people about you," McCarthy said.

"Let's just say I'm here to advise you on the group's financial structure, as you suggested over the phone. It's the truth and—"

McCarthy was shaking his head. "That'll give too much away. They'll smell a rat as soon as you start asking questions. These guys blab anything and everything to the press. Let's say you're with another outfit in San Diego, or something, and you want to see how we're set up."

Now it was Henry's turn to shake his head. They bantered

back and forth for a while, Henry indicating his new-found moral disdain of phony covers, and McCarthy insisting on secrecy as the greater good. It wasn't resolved until Henry started talking about the 1:45 Amtrak that could take him back home.

McCarthy stepped back, screwed up the corners of his mouth to indicate disgust, and sighed, "Okay, okay. But let's stress the advisory angle, and keep it as discreet as possible. C'mon, I want you to see the center."

They walked back to the car and started on their way again in virtual silence. Henry wondered about the guilt feelings he was experiencing. Suppose there was a theft, and the press got ahold of it, and suppose Vern McCarthy was to blame for the Center's demise. Perhaps he should have offered to bend. Did he really have the right to force his morals on others' careers and desires? If he was going to continue to live in the world with other human beings, and have commercial and social intercourse, he would need to make some allowances. But how would he draw the line? He tried to think of the few passages of Scripture he knew, to see if something might help in the situation, but nothing came to mind. One more problem to put on his prayer list: to be the company's man, or your own man and thereby God's, or a combination thereof.

As they rounded an unusually tight bend in the road, Henry sneaked a glance at the pursed-lipped McCarthy. He realized again how far he had to go in his Christian growth, for he felt no love for the energetic little man next to him. On the other hand, he would try to do him no harm.

"There it is," McCarthy announced with all his old enthusiasm. The chaparral and scrub oak they had been driving through abruptly stopped as they passed through a low cement and stone wall surrounding a gently sloping mesa.

The new winding blacktop road was lined with Italian cyprus, which Henry estimated to be about ten years old. They wound through a landscaped parking lot with well-manicured patches of lawns, graced with trees and shrubs foreign to the countryside. If money really was tight, the gardeners didn't know it.

The main building loomed before them much larger than

Henry had expected from the overlooking hillside, an illusion no doubt created by the monolithic nature of the design. Huge slabs, made of smooth river-bottom rocks jutting through light brown mortar, were prowed unevenly together, angling away from the viewer and giving the building a fortress-like appearance. For some reason unknown to him, Henry thought of Orson Welles and Great Dane dogs.

The car swung quickly around the back of the building, then jerked to a halt. Henry pushed himself off the dashboard; he had been gazing at the building and didn't see the small Japanese pickup ahead of them.

"Hey, you're in my parking place!" McCarthy shouted out the window.

A thick-set workman with tar-stained coveralls and black mustache rose out of the pickup. "You danged right I'm in your place." He grasped a small vial of liquid in his hand which he held up to show McCarthy, but McCarthy whirled his car around and swung into an adjoining slot.

"Impudent fool!" he muttered, hopping out of the car and calling for Henry to follow. He hurried along the walkway toward his office. The workman was soon at his heels, but McCarthy didn't stop.

"If you want to see me, you can make an appointment like everybody else," he grumbled.

"I been trying to get an appointment with you an' you dang well know it," the workman growled, while trying to keep pace with McCarthy. Again he thrust the vial toward McCarthy, but McCarthy agilely slid by the man, through the large glass door, and disappeared inside.

The workman considered following, but turned and faced Henry coming up the walk.

"You work here, do you?" he blurted.

"What's on your mind?" Henry asked.

McCarthy reappeared at the door. "C'mon, Henry, I want to show you something." Henry gestured he would be right along, but when it became evident he intended to hear out the workman, McCarthy disappeared again.

"Read that. Just read that," he insisted, shoving his evidence at Henry.

There was a small green slip of paper taped to the side of the vial, and Henry had to put on his reading glasses to read the small writing. It looked like a lab analysis report. The words "iodine" and "chlorine" were underlined.

"Could be drinking water," Henry said. "So?"

"Well," the workman snorted, his finger wagging in Henry's face, "you're a very smart fellow. And do you know where I got that water? From under your roof where there's s'posed to be a leak!" He waved skyward toward the top of the building. "Somebody's been playing little tricks on me so I don't gotta be paid. So I hid little bowls up there where the rain is s'posed to come through. When it rained last month, I got this instead of rain water. Now I don't like goin' to court but by golly—"

"You're the roofing contractor?"

"Sure. What else would I be?"

"I'm Henry Garrott," Henry said, extending his hand. The gesture seemed to subdue the man.

"Bixby. Haniford and Bixby Construction."

"When did you do the roofing job?"

"Thirteen months ago. Now I admit, we had some problems at first. This building wasn't designed right in the first place, and we had the same problems the builder had. We aren't making a cent on this job, but when we had that last heavy rain this spring, I found spray patterns up there like someone took a garden hose and sprayed water around up under the ceiling."

"Have you been paid for any of your work?"

"Not a cent. We guarantee our work, but I sure don't plan on waiting till it rains again next fall for the pay."

"We have your bill?"

"You got *five* copies of the bill."

"Well, Mr. Bixby, you've leveled a very serious charge against someone in the institution, or the institution itself. I'm not in a position to act on this myself, but I'll certainly bring it to the attention of Mr. McCarthy. Do you have any way to verify where this water came from, other than your own word?"

Bixby scratched his nose. "Well, my partner's son was along and Hal what's-his-name, a journeyman roofer we use."

"It might also be a good idea to get some pictures of the water stains, if you can."

"Pictures?"

"Anything to indicate the water was the result of spraying from the inside rather than normal leakage patterns."

Henry handed back the vial and bid the surprised Bixby good-bye, leaving him at the entrance scratching his head.

Inside the building Henry wandered through a labyrinth of storage rooms and small offices filled with lab equipment in various stages of unpacking and storage. Excelsior and Styrofoam packing bubbles were scattered about in the hallways as well as in several of the rooms.

"May I help you?" a young feminine voice called from behind.

Henry turned to see a girl in a beige smock, her hair pulled back. The large eyeglasses, the pencil behind the ear, and a large amber glass bulb in her hands, still dripping excelsior, told him she was someone's lab assistant.

"Ah, yes. I was with Mr. McCarthy. We just arrived, but apparently I got left behind."

"His office is through there on the other side of the main hall." She gestured with her head.

"Thank you."

"Be careful where you walk. We're working in there."

"Yes, I will," Henry said and started following her directions. The double doors labelled "Great Hall" at the end of the corridor opened into a large room, towering some four stories high and crowned with a golden dome. Encircling the dome was an inscription: "THE WISE APPLICATION OF KNOWLEDGE IS MAN'S GRANDEST ACHIEVEMENT" (Gen. C. J. Kilbourne).

Maneuvering himself around to read the inscription, Henry bumped his leg against a bulb similar to the one he had seen in the girl's hands, except this one was a deep burgundy. He picked it up and found it to be surprisingly light; it was shaped like a football, only larger, with large screw holes in each end. The sunshine transmitted through the object created an eerie, visual opulence Henry found hard to look at for any length of time.

In the center of the Great Hall, descending directly below

the dome, were two spiraling chains of the same bulbs—some square, some T-shaped, others L-shaped, and all in a myriad of colors. There were interlocking thick plastic chains between the spirals and guy wires and metal shafts, acting as braces, extending in many directions. In several spots, the chains were incomplete. Two men in light blue smocks stood on top of a scaffolding, some thirty-five feet high, assembling the structure.

Henry considered the color selections a bit deficient for a work of art. He returned the bulb to its nest of packing material and began wending his way across the room, among packing boxes and around the scaffolding. He turned toward the two figures on the scaffold as their voices rose in anger. They were silhouetted against the sun streaming through the large ocean-view windows. The effect of the bright coastal haze and the sun shining through the colored prisms gave Henry a distinct sense of danger, a sense of having lived through this experience before, but he couldn't recall what happened next.

He started backing up while keeping his eye on the men. Because of the echo in the room and overlapping shouts, most of their words were lost to him. He did catch: " . . . but I tell you your sequence is wrong." " . . . my area of specialty. . . . You dare to tell me my area of specialty . . . " "Give it to me . . . Not there, I tell you, not there!"

One of the larger prisms they had been arguing over tumbled from their grasp and before they could recover it, it rolled off the platform, sailing toward Henry. Ready for it, Henry sidestepped quickly; but the falling missile struck a support wire and bounded toward his feet, striking the marble floor and shattering with a terrible racket. Henry went sprawling on the floor among the clattering, scraping orange fragments.

"Good heavens, man! Are you all right?" one man on the scaffold called, then started quickly down the ladder.

Henry chuckled nervously and rose to his feet, more embarrassed than hurt. "Yes, I think so. Just my hand." He had cut the soft heel of his left hand and began dabbing it with his handkerchief.

"You're bleeding," the descending man said. He was a tall mulatto in his early forties. "Shall I take a look at that? I'm a medical doctor." He took Henry's hand and started examining it without waiting for an answer.

"Medical doctor? You do objets d'art in your spare time, do you?"

"Art? Oh, this." He laughed. "No, no, this is a DNA model. This was designed by the big artist in the sky."

"That's a matter of conjecture," said the plump man on the scaffolding. He had come half way down and seated himself to light a cigarette. "Do you think he's going to live?"

"I'm Dr. Robinson," the mulatto said. "The sarcastic gentleman on the steps is Professor Shoemaker."

"How do you do," Henry said, then grunted with pain from Dr. Robinson's probing.

"I think you have a piece of plastic imbedded in there."

Henry flexed his hand and did his own examination and said, "Oh, I don't think so."

"What's all the racket?" Vern McCarthy yelled, storming out of his office. "Oh, no! Not another element."

"The $250 variety this time," Professor Shoemaker said.

"Well, we're not replacing it."

"We have to replace it," Shoemaker whined.

"You'll just have to work around it. When it's finished, we'll get a local glass blower to make the missing pieces. He's got to be cheaper." McCarthy scuffed at some of the pieces at his feet. "What are you men doing on that rickety scaffolding anyway? We have maintenance staff for that work."

"I was giving Dr. Robinson a lesson in simple genetics," Shoemaker sneered.

"Very funny," Robinson said.

"C'mon, Henry," McCarthy said gruffly, and started toward his office with Henry in tow.

"Better have that looked after," Robinson said.

"Yes, I will."

"Who's your friend?" Shoemaker called.

"Oh, this is Henry Garrott," McCarthy mumbled. "He's a friend of mine here to . . . " McCarthy cleared his throat and found some more orange plastic fragments to kick. "Dr. Robinson, better get someone in here to get this cleaned up right away."

"Yes, we will."

"Don't want any more accidents," McCarthy grumbled and escorted Henry into his office.

Shoemaker watched them disappear, then raised an eyebrow for Robinson's benefit. "Now, what's he doing here?"

"With my *inferior* intellect, how would I know? I jes' sweeps de flo an mins ma own bin'ness," Robinson intoned, shuffling off toward the storage area.

Shoemaker smiled and called after him. "Bitter, bitter."

"Miss Matthews, would you see about a Band-Aid or something for Mr. Garrott's hand?"

"Oh my, yes," Miss Matthews said. She impressed Henry as the epitome of a career secretary now nearing the end of her working years. She rose and started about her task as McCarthy and Henry passed through the outer office and into the Administrator's plush facilities. "And maybe some coffee too, please," McCarthy called back.

His office, like the main hall, was designed for maximum impact on people impressed with architecture. The vaulted ceiling, the splendid westerly view of the ocean, the abrupt cliffs, and rolling green hills seemed to inspire lofty thoughts. Henry, more impressed with the practical, noticed that the ornate doorknobs were too high for the short McCarthy, and the chairs around the low conference table looked very uninviting for his own long legs. Somebody, in an effort to impress the human spirit, forgot about the human body.

McCarthy folded back a wall panel and a light went on over a hidden washstand. "Rinse your hand in here."

As Henry washed up, McCarthy seated himself behind his large desk and started thumbing his mail. "Did you and the roofer have a nice chat?"

Henry smiled. "I suppose you know what he wanted."

"He wants his money."

"Do you know what he has in that bottle?"

"Haven't the foggiest."

"How long did you say you knew about the money missing?"

McCarthy slapped down a large envelope hard enough to

let Henry know he was irritated. "Just like I told you over the phone. I just found out about it."

Miss Matthews appeared with a tray of coffee, then helped Henry apply a Band-Aid to the cut. This gave Henry a moment to evaluate McCarthy's response. There was a trace too much irritation in his voice; if he hadn't sprayed water in the rafters, Henry felt sure he knew about the roofer's charge.

"Miss Matthews, do you have a car key for Mr. Garrott?"

"No sir, the rental agency said the car would have to be picked up at the filling station."

"We just came from town! Why didn't you tell me this before?"

Miss Matthews crisply put down the coffee pot she had started pouring from, walked to the front of McCarthy's desk and pointed to a small pink memo that was on his blotter; then, in a quiet but firm voice, said, "I gave you this note yesterday afternoon at 2:30, explaining they couldn't deliver the car as you requested."

"Oh." McCarthy read and crumpled the note. "Well, I guess I missed it."

Miss Matthews returned to pouring coffee without a trace of the smile Henry thought she deserved. McCarthy outlined Henry's itinerary: He had reserved a room for Henry at the Hyatt House in town. And McCarthy and his wife would be pleased to have him come to dinner at their home that evening—they would be dining with the Ballards. "We try to meet socially with each of the full-timers from time to time, and tonight it's the Ballards."

Henry said he would be delighted to join them.

There was more small talk—about the poor service one can expect in small towns, the type car they had rented for Henry's use, and the weather turning warmer—until Miss Matthews had finished the traditional secretarial duties and left the room. McCarthy then unlocked a low cabinet behind his desk and produced two ledger books—one large and one small, both crammed with loose papers. "Matthews is part of the old guard around here. Used to work for Kilbourne himself. I haven't figured her out yet, so the less she knows about all this, the better."

McCarthy slid the books across the desk. "Here're all our records. And I have an appointment for you at the bank with Mister Lipert at two o'clock this afternoon."

"He's the president?"

"Well, he's the manager. I don't know what his title is. Really a weird duck. I put the fear of God into him the other day. Accused him of everything from embezzling to running a sleazy slip-shod outfit. He's supposed to be double-checking all his records and should have some answers for you."

McCarthy pulled out a drawer, propped his small feet up, and smirked. "I told him you were with the Government, and were here expressly to look into his banking procedures."

Henry flinched noticeably. "You know, Vernon, I really don't like your methods."

"Listen, you've gotta take a few liberties with these small town slowpokes. Otherwise, you'll never get anything done." McCarthy gulped some coffee and scanned his ocean view. "At least he won't start talking to the press."

Henry had expected to develop a rapport with McCarthy, but it wasn't happening, and it puzzled him. There was a posturing aloofness about him that hadn't been evident in Europe.

Miss Matthews broke in on the intercom with the message that Professor Shoemaker was driving into the village and would be happy to drop Mr. Garrott off at the filling station. This flustered McCarthy, for he wanted Henry to take the books with him and study them over the weekend. Since he couldn't very well carry them around in plain view, they rummaged around in a small supply room next door and came up with a scruffy-looking, old leather briefcase into which McCarthy jammed the ledgers, crumpling many of the loose papers in the process.

Henry was hurried outside and bid a half-hearted good-bye to McCarthy—only to be left standing in the wrong parking lot, waiting for his ride. Miss Matthews finally had to correct the error and escort Henry to Shoemaker's car on the other side of the building. The confusion continued as they attempted to retrieve Henry's luggage from the Mercedes.

"Surely these people can't be some of the best minds in the nation," Henry said to himself. "This must just be a bad day for them." The disorderliness and poor personal communication dismayed Henry, and he looked forward to better days.

Prof. Shoemaker chain-smoked all the way into town and amicably tried to coax information out of Henry. He could have been the model for the saying, "Inside every fat man there is a thin man trying to get out." He was thin-boned, with delicate facial features, but great globs of puffy fat pulled down his jowls and protruded over his belt. His quick mind and animated gestures seemed to put him in direct and constant conflict with the lardy inertia of his mass.

"Are you planning to be at the Center long?" Shoemaker asked, while simultaneously attempting to remove his suit coat, adjust the radio, flick the ashes off his cigarette, and negotiate a tight corner at maximum speed. Henry didn't answer immediately; he was busy applying the imaginary brake pedal beneath his right foot.

Shoemaker went on, "Not too much happening at the Center right now. Getting ready for the press conference next week. You down for that?"

"No," Henry grimaced, giving a good imitation of Don Knotts.

Shoemaker's right cuff link had gotten caught in his coat sleeve lining and he began flopping about like a wounded duck. Henry quickly came to his aid, then more shoving and wedging ensued as the Professor pried his coat out from behind himself and tossed it into the back seat. All through this, he expounded on the incongruity of the expensive and aloof Center, juxtaposed with the languishing artist colony and fishing village.

Henry heard little of what he said; it had always been difficult for him to concentrate on two things at once, especially when one involved personal safety. Just as the last hairpin turn was made and the big white Oldsmobile slowed to accommodate the streets of Almaden, Henry felt he could relax. As though on cue, the radio burst forth with a familiar Christian chorus, "Let's Just Praise the Lord." This was a song his group in Washington had often sung, and Henry smiled at its appropriateness and mouthed the words along with the radio singers.

Shoemaker whirled the knob to another station. "Blasted,

ubiquitous religious broadcasters. Now they're polluting the FM band, too."

"I was rather enjoying it," Henry volunteered.

Shoemaker flicked off the radio and chuckled in an attempt to change the subject. "Okay, I give up. What are you in town for?"

"Is it so important to you?"

"Well, we all have our axes to grind," Shoemaker mumbled, lighting up a new Winston from the last butt. "I had you pegged for a scientific journalist, but that can't be right. You didn't even recognize our DNA model. Plus, you like religious music."

"I don't follow."

"What scientist in his right mind goes around humming tunes of that palaver?"

"Oh, I didn't realize the two were incompatible—being a scientist and a hymn hummer."

Shoemaker laughed again. "Religion simply has no relevancy in today's world. As the kids say, 'It isn't where it's at.' Why mess about with empirical theories when there are worlds to conquer. We're on the verge of breakthroughs that will change the way millions of people live—but I'm changing the subject. Is there some dark, mysterious reason why you can't explain your presence at the Center?"

"No, I don't think so. I'm here to advise the Director on some financial matters."

"Oh." Shoemaker seemed disappointed.

"Does that relieve your mind?"

Shoemaker chuckled and his belly shook. "Listen, I know I'm not the most popular person in Camelot. I just don't want McCarthy bringing in a ringer on me."

"A ringer? What would a 'ringer' be?" Henry queried.

"Never mind. I just like to keep all the bases covered." He did seem relieved and the conversation turned to lighter subjects until they neared the filling station with the rental cars.

"Sorry about the information-pumping," Shoemaker admitted as Henry gathered his gear. "If I can help you in any way, let me know."

"Thanks for the offer and the lift," Henry said. "Goodbye."

The big Olds sped down the street toward the next stop sign. Henry vowed not to get himself in a situation where he would have to ride with him again.

He checked out his nondescript little Fairmont, drove to a sandwich shop for a bite of lunch, and found he still had time to check into his room before his two o'clock appointment with Lipert.

At his motel room desk, he sorted through the ledgers for pertinent information that might help at the bank, then plopped on the bed and called home.

"Henry, I thought you'd wait and call this evening after the rates change!" Valery exclaimed.

"I meant to, dear, but I want to call Becky and I took off without her number. Would you look it up for me?"

"Of course." There was a pause while Valery looked up their daughter's number; she came back on the line with the question Henry knew was inevitable:

"What do you need to talk to Becky about?"

Henry explained his need for some information in her major field of study—biological sciences. This satisfied Valery's curiosity; the number was given and more pleasantries were exchanged.

Henry said, "I won't call again until tomorrow since you now know I've reached my destination safely."

She reminded him that this was Becky's first finals week, and heaven knows where she might be.

But Becky was in her dorm and immediately came to the phone when her father called.

"Daddy?"

"Yes, it's me."

"Is everything all right?"

"Oh, yes, I wanted to call and say 'good luck' on your finals . . ."

"Oh, they're all over but one, but thanks."

" . . . and to start getting my money back from all this education."

Becky laughed hesitantly. "What do you mean?"

"Can you explain to me, in layman's terms, what DNA is?"

"Daddy, honestly, everybody knows that."

"Well, after you tell me, then maybe everyone *will* know. I know it's something like a code in the human body."

"That's right. It's in every cell of every living organism, we think. DNA stands for deoxyribonucleic acid, and it's a series of amino acids and stuff that is actually the key to all genetic traits, and really the whole physical makeup of the organism. It's fantastic. It makes you stop and wonder about life and all, you know?"

"Yes, it does," Henry agreed.

"And the cells in all multi-cellular organisms multiply by dividing. You follow me? You see, the DNA is in the form of two chains, sort of coiled together—"

"Like a double helix?"

"Right," Becky approved like a proud teacher. "Say, you catch on in a hurry, Daddy."

"Well, I've seen a model of something like that."

"That's gotta be something to see! I mean, even the DNA of a simple virus has over a thousand parts. Anyway, back to the dividing cell. When the cell is ready to split, the DNA helix separates like an untwining rope, and the two separate chains find new partners, because RNA, another substance in the cell, goes around hunting for the right amino acids to join onto the split DNA spirals—and you end up with two identical DNA helixes; and the cell divides again."

"I think you lost me in there with the RNA."

"Well, I don't understand it all either," Becky conceded. "The chemical activity that goes on inside those little teeny cells before it divides is just mind-boggling.

"You know," she continued after a philosophical pause, "when I came to college I really didn't know if I believed in God or not; and I was sure college would be a religious wipe-out. But you know, it's been just the opposite. I mean, if there's such order and meaning and all in life, there *has* to be a mind behind it all. There's no way these things could happen just by chance. You know?"

"Yes . . . yes, I know." Henry was smiling to himself.

"And Daddy, Mom told me about what happened to you—what you've been through—your conversion and all."

"I didn't realize that. I planned on telling you this summer when you were home from your trip."

"I hope it's all right that Mom told me—"

"Yes, it's all right. Don't worry about it."

"Because I think it's just great—to make a commitment like that in your advanced years—"

"Advanced years!" Henry exclaimed with mock surprise.

"Well, middle-aged years. I think it's very exciting. And it seems right, too, you know? I mean if there is an intelligent, caring mind behind the universe, it makes sense that he would be like the God of the Bible. I mean, caring and loving people on earth. Am I making sense?"

"You certainly are," Henry faltered. His eyes were moist, and he paused, steadying his voice. "I'm very happy to hear you say that. You and I are going to have a lot to talk about this summer."

Becky gave a quick laugh of agreement and another long pause followed as father and daughter cemented a new-found bond of friendship over three thousand miles of telephone line.

"How come you're asking about DNA, Daddy?"

"I'm doing some work for the Kilbourne people here on the coast."

"Oh, of course—"

"You've heard of them?"

"Dr. Begelman did one of my current textbooks. And there's a Professor Ballard out there too."

"What's the nature of their work? Do you know? I get the feeling they're on the verge of some big announcement. Are they active in this cloning business?"

"Not that I know of," Becky said. "I know Ballard has been researching the effects of viruses on human cells."

"Hmmm. All of which is quite expensive, I suppose. I wish I knew more about biology. I may have to call you again if I get stuck and need an expert. I better ring off now."

"Okay, sounds great. Sounds a bit mysterious too."

"Bye, darling."

"Bye, Daddy."

Henry glanced at his watch and made a quick phone call to the weather information officer at the nearby Air Force Base. The last prolonged rain of any significance fell twenty-three days ago, on May 15 to 17.

He found the bank without any problem, and following an old habit, he drove two and a half blocks farther, parked the car, and doubled back toward the bank on foot, absorbing a bit of the local color on the way.

Several of the shops displayed paintings and other assorted pieces of art, from the local colony, in their display windows. He noticed two very attractive renderings of the local cannery and the fishing boats in the harbor; before he left, he would have to do some serious shopping for the walls of their new home. He studied the price tags; most items were quite reasonable. Surprisingly reasonable, he decided. Business must be slow.

It wasn't until then he noticed the early signs of dilapidation in the streets of this quaint little fishing village-art community. A torn awning, a few vacant stores, and two-week-old litter in the gutters. The two trash receptacles he passed were both in need of repair. If Henry had to make an educated guess, he would say the fair village of Almaden was on the skids.

Henry slipped on his coat and entered the small one-story building on the corner labeled "Almaden Commercial Bank: We're here to satisfy your banking needs."

"Mr. Lipert is expecting you, sir," the plump, middle-aged lady with small pince-nez glasses informed. "He's in his office right over there."

Henry gave a courtesy rap on the glass portion of the door and entered. Gilbert Lipert, his hand over the mouthpiece of his phone, pointed at a chair. "I won't be a moment," he whispered.

Henry sat down in the chair indicated and glanced about the room while waiting. Mr. Lipert, it appeared, was one of the long-standing participants in the local art fair poetry contests. A second place ribbon and two honorable mention plaques adorned the wall behind his desk and were surrounded by several framed poems bearing his signature.

Mr. Lipert himself was desperately in need of a new hairpiece. His receding bald spot peeked quite obviously from under the back part of his toupee. And the false hair had not greyed along with his real hair.

"Well-ll, Mr. Garrott, I presume," Mr. Lipert enthused as he hung up his phone.

"Yes, it's good of you to see me."

"Not at all," Lipert answered, shaking hands very formally.

"I'd first of all like to correct any misinformation you might have as to my being here: I do not work for the Government."

"Oh, goodness, I know that." Lipert waved the matter away, demonstrating a surprisingly loose wrist for a banker. "Your Mr. McCarthy is quite easy to see through, if you don't mind my saying so. We are an old, well-established firm in the community, and we are not in the habit of falling apart whenever a client makes an emotional charge."

Henry thought of reminding him of the size of the account of this particular client, but decided to keep it cool.

"I see your point. Mr. Lipert, I'm an accountant and have been hired by the Kilbourne Group, through Mr. McCarthy, to advise them regarding their financial picture. Now the matter of most immediate concern is their general operating fund."

"Of course. I've warned them repeatedly about their careless handling of such large sums of money. I dare say old Kilbourne would be turning over in his grave if he knew of this latest fiasco."

"Fiasco? I think that's a rather strong term," Henry protested.

This seemed to open the floodgates for Lipert. As Henry asked questions pertinent to the general fund, Lipert used each occasion to add gossipy tidbits about the Kilbourne Group and their troubles with the community. Among other things, Henry learned that Gen. Kilbourne had tried to establish a strong rapport between his scientists and the artists of Almaden. There had even been something of a scandal when it was discovered three artists with good west-coast credentials had been paid by Kilbourne to move to Almaden Village. "As though artists were like football players who can be bought and sold," Lipert scoffed. "We are not a provincial community, Mr. Garrott, but it soon became evident to those Kilbourne people that they were not wanted here."

Henry marvelled at the man's inconsistencies assuring him this was not a provincial town, and in his very next breath proving it was precisely that.

Henry smiled and searched his mind for a way to get out of Lipert what he wanted. When he commented on the poetry awards on the wall, Lipert displayed appropriate modesty, but then responded with pride to the flattery. He spoke of the poetry reading clubs he had formed locally and the great avenues of pleasure his avocation had afforded him.

Finally, after a pause in Lipert's ramblings, Henry ventured, "I wonder, Mr. Lipert, if you could help me on one point?"

"What might that be?"

"I suppose it's obvious to you, but I don't seem to grasp it. Why do you think the people of Almaden have not taken kindly to the Kilbourne Center? I would think most communities would consider it an asset."

"That's because you weren't here in the beginning. Twelve years ago they came in here with all their grand-di-ose ideas about building the ideal community of great minds. They were going to get Sacramento to put the new freeway through here. Why, we even gave 'em the land that . . . that . . . ugly fortress stands on."

"Freeway? What freeway is that?"

"Why Kilbourne was supposed to have all kinds of connections in Washington and Sacramento, and the Belton Freeway was supposed to come through here. It was part of the deal. Once our county supervisors were committed, and *they* started building their"—Lipert had difficulty saying the word— "center, we got word from the Highway Department the freeway was going inland through Manning in order to save money. And what do we get? The lousy Amtrak train that nobody rides; and all the tourist trade goes down to Laguna, or somewhere else."

"I see," Henry sympathized. It was apparent he had struck a nerve. "It seems General Kilbourne didn't have as much influence as people thought."

"Listen, there are many people in this town that think he

never intended to have that freeway through here. They're not dependent on it for their livelihood. Why should they care? They sit up there in their ivory tower getting those big government contracts." He fumed in silence for a moment, then swung his chair around to face Henry.

"But alas, alas. The enterprises of great pith and moment turned awry."

Lipert smiled benevolently and changed his tone. "You asked about their general fund. You'll find everything in order." He opened a folder on his desk and began showing items to Henry as he referred to them.

"Here is the signature card. Each check must have two signatures in order to be valid—the acting treasurer and one other. I've made photostats of all their major checks for the last year from our microfilm. I believe you'll find everything in order. These balance statements no doubt are duplicates of the ones you have in your briefcase."

Lipert interlaced his fingers and watched Henry absorb the material.

"Sooo . . . from a year ago their balance has gone from $1,326,000 to $3,700."

"As of this morning's posting, that is correct."

"There is one name on this signature card I don't recognize—the treasurer, Bertha E. Corbut."

"Mr. Garrott, don't play games with me."

"Games? Should I know the woman?" Henry asked blankly.

"We had no idea the woman was dead. It's certainly not our fault. The first cancelled check should have told them something was wrong."

"Wait a minute, wait a minute," Henry blurted. "You mean you cleared some of these checks after this woman died?"

"We didn't learn of her death until your McCarthy told us."

"When was that?"

Lipert rubbed his palms. "Last week."

"And when did she die?"

"Last February."

"Good heavens!"

"She passed away in Cleveland. The only local obituary listed her under her married name, Bertha Fenner," Lipert said, dabbing lightly at his palms with his folded handkerchief. "And that was a small notice in the Los Angeles paper. I'm sure you'll find the bank followed all the proper procedures."

"I see . . ." Henry mused.

He was busily flipping through the checks when Lipert stood up, indicating the interview was at an end.

"May I keep this signature card?" Henry asked.

"I'm sure you understand we need that for our records. I'll be happy to make a copy for you. You might also remind your Mr. McCarthy this account is closed until a new signature card is signed. He better get his people in here to sign the new one. Good-bye, Mr. Garrott. And good luck."

There was another oddity about the checks which Henry didn't share with Lipert. He hurried back to his motel room to verify his suspicions. Taping the check copy with the most current date against the window he began overlaying the older checks one by one against the taped master, lining up each one to compare the "Bertha E. Corbut" signatures. There were normal variations in all of the signatures before December, but beginning December 15 forward, all of the signatures were identical. Since no one signs his name exactly the same each time, the checks dating December forward must have been done with a signature stamp.

He then spread the check copies in question before him on the desk. There were twelve in all. Adding the numbers quickly in his mind, he came up with something around $700,000, not the one million McCarthy had claimed was missing. What do you buy for $700,000 these days if you are a supposedly honest highly dedicated research scientist? . . . or a small town bank officer? How much do new hairpieces cost? When the checks were again placed in date sequence another pattern emerged:

Date	Cosigner	Issued to
December 15	F. Begelman	Malloy Pharmaceutical Supply

December 22	F. Begelman	Malloy Pharmaceutical Supply
January 13	F. Begelman	Malloy Pharmaceutical Supply
January 20	J. Ballard	Hubbard/Teague Surgical Supply
January 23	A. K. Shoemaker	Computers Plus
January 27	J. Ballard	Computers Plus
February 27	Marion D. Jones	Midwest Advertisers Service
February 27	Marion D. Jones	Midwest Advertisers Service
March 3	Marion D. Jones	Midwest Advertisers Service
April 12	F. Begelman	Malloy Pharmaceutical Supply
May 1	F. Begelman	Malloy Pharmaceutical Supply
May 12	J. Ballard	Computers Plus

With the one exception of J. Ballard, all the cosigners were lumped in time groups. Very unusual, unless of course . . .

Henry plopped on the bed again, dialed the Center and asked to speak to Miss Matthews.

"Yes, Mr. Garrott. How may I help you?"

"I was wondering if you keep track of staff vacation schedules and the like," Henry asked.

"Well, not really. Regular staff members are quite independent. They don't have to answer to anyone."

"But you would, as a rule, know where a staff member is at any one given time. Don't some of them ask you to make plane reservations, and so on?"

There was a pause at the other end of the line as Miss Matthews had second thoughts about her offer to help. "I'm not so sure this is the type of information you should be . . . I'm not in the habit of spying."

"Miss Matthews, you know I'm working under the auspices of Mr. McCarthy."

"Yes."

"And I assure you I have the best interests of the Center at heart. I'm not asking to know where anyone travels to when they are away from the Center. I simply want to know when certain individuals have been away from the Center or the vicinity for an extended period."

"Well . . . "

"Any employer or management team has the right to such information. For instance, was Dr. Begelman in residence last December . . . say from December 15 through January 13?"

"Dr. Begelman suffered a stroke last December, the early part of December. He still does most of his work at home."

"And that lady that died in Cleveland, Bertha Corbut, had she been away from the Center since December?"

"Ahh, yes, I believe she had. She and Dr. Jones were working on a presentation in December and January which required their being away."

Henry continued down the list; each cosigner had been away from the Center during, or shortly after, the time their checks were clearing. That is, with the exception of J. Ballard.

Miss Matthews warmed up considerably as Henry's questions demonstrated such remarkable accuracy. By the time they concluded, she was quite cordial. He was glad about that, for she could be an invaluable source of information.

Rather than mull over everything then, Henry decided to give his subconscious a crack at it. He cleared his mind as best he could, stripped to his shorts and went through his calisthenics routine with determination.

In the shower, with the hot pulses from the shower rippling on his tired back, Henry tried to fit the pieces together. Whoever tapped the funds had to know whose names were on that signature card, the activities of the different signatories, and more than that, he or she must have known no one was tending the store. As for the water sprayed under the roof, they must have known the roofing bill was scheduled to be paid from this account. He would have to double-check and find out if this was true.

And the companies those checks were written to . . . no doubt phony fronts used to clear the funds. . . . But will double-check with old friend Hubert in L.A. accounting office in a.m. on legitimacy of company names. But tomorrow's Saturday . . .

J. Ballard and wife are scheduled to be at McCarthy's dinner party . . . would like to question him casually before he knows about suspicions . . . must get there early so McCarthy doesn't tip him off. What was he thinking? McCarthy was the one that wanted his activities kept sub rosa. What a stupid slip.

Henry was overwhelmed with the feeling that he was getting in over his head. There was intelligence, energy, and purpose behind these actions, and no doubt, criminal intent. The thing to do was to persuade McCarthy to turn the matter over to the police, or the FBI, since bank fraud, especially interstate bank fraud, fell under their jurisdiction. But would Vern listen to reason?

After Henry dressed for the dinner party, he sat by the window with his long legs propped up on the desk. He found his place in the Psalms: "Why dost thou stand at a distance, O Lord? Why dost thou hide thyself in times of trouble? In arrogance the wicked hotly pursue the afflicted; let them be taken in the schemes which they have devised."

If McCarthy's home wasn't the best house in town, it must have been a close second. The simple, stark white gables and columns of Early American design seemed out of place, after the many blocks of red Spanish tile and brown adobe. Like the Center, it was set on the crest of a hill and offered a pleasant, although not as spectacular, view of the ocean and village below.

Henry pulled his Fairmont into the combination driveway-courtyard and parked behind the two Mercedes in the open garage. In the third stall of the three-car garage, a red-headed, bespectacled youngster was whirling about frantically on his plastic Big Wheel and shouting wildly, "The Katzenjammer Kids! The Katzenjammer Kids!"

McCarthy's wife, Millie, greeted him warmly at the front

door and introduced herself. At first glance Henry thought she must be Vern's sister because she bore such a strong physical resemblance to her husband. She was a plump little lady, and the straight, floor-length hostess outfit she wore didn't do much to diminish her figure.

Henry found McCarthy in the kitchen pantry, cracking chunks off a clump of ice. "Stupid maid," he grumbled, "let the chipped ice start to melt, then tried to refreeze it."

As McCarthy chiseled off the ice slivers, he dropped them into the bottom halves of two-piece crystal goblets sitting on the pantry shelf. Apparently they were going to have chilled shrimp cocktails with their dinner.

He continued his task as Henry pulled up a stool and tried to bring him up-to-date on what he had discovered. McCarthy worked on, giving no indication of surprise or dismay at Henry's bad news. When Henry expressed his wish to turn the matter over to the authorities, McCarthy shook his head firmly from side to side.

"I told you before, we can't have that kind of publicity now. No matter how discreet they promise to be, word always gets out."

"This government contract you're waiting for—are you sure it's all that important?" Henry asked.

"It only means the future of the Center."

Henry slapped his knees and rose to pace. "Well, I don't know what else I can do for you. We'll need additional help tracing down these companies the checks were written to. That'll mean a team of private investigators in Cleveland and—"

McCarthy was shaking his head again. "I don't have that kind of money."

"Then what is it you want?"

"I want you to find out who it is that's doing this and expose—well, don't even expose them. Just let me know who it is."

"About all I can do is start questioning people, and if I do that, it's just a matter of time before they start putting two-and-two together. People are going to find out about this. It's inevitable."

"It seems to me we had this conversation once before," McCarthy growled, jabbing at the unresponsive ice. "Frankly, I thought you'd be a little further along by now. Don't you have any idea who it might be?"

"Who was on your selection committee that supported you for this position?"

"I have no way of knowing who did or didn't support my candidacy. Why?"

"I thought perhaps someone knew you were weak on finance and wanted you in this position for that very reason," Henry said. "If we could put the names of your selection committee supporters in a computer, along with the names of the people on the signature card and others cognizant of the banking procedures, we could begin narrowing this down to some prime suspects."

McCarthy wasn't listening. "Who says I'm weak on finances? Finance wasn't even mentioned in the interview. Why, one of the reasons I got this job was because they knew I'd be a strong fund-raiser. A *strong* fund-raiser."

Furiously, McCarthy slammed the ice pick at the ice ball. The ice scooted off the butcher block table and spun defiantly into the far corner of the room.

What manner of man is this, Henry pondered, watching McCarthy fumble for the frozen orb. The ancient Greeks had a saying: "If the gods wish to destroy a man, they start by making him angry." All the energies that used to drive McCarthy's buoyant enthusiasms seemed to be turning to frustrated anger. He even misunderstood the reference to finance. Was he going to come crashing down and bring Henry down with him? And why this display of east coast elegance in the midst of California casual? Chilled shrimp cocktail in crystal goblets, indeed! Henry longed for more distance between himself and his client.

"Was the roof repair bill scheduled to be paid out of the general fund?"

"We have a maintenance account. But there isn't . . ." McCarthy took a quick glance at Henry. "Yes. I have a choice. I can pay some on the roofing bill, or pay you."

"I see." Henry shuffled and McCarthy chipped. "I'm

afraid I won't be able to work for nothing, Vern."

"But don't you see? When we recover the money, there'll be no problem."

"Afraid I can't work that way. I have two children in college—"

"Where am I supposed to get the money?"

"You could always sell one of your Mercedes."

Henry had meant it as a joke, to lighten a suddenly heavy conversation, but when he saw the incredulous burning stare in McCarthy's eyes, he decided not to smile back.

"All right, all right," McCarthy said finally. "I'll get you a retainer check Monday morning. What happened to all those Christian principles you were spouting off about over the phone . . . Help your fellowman, and all that?"

"Oh, they're still there. Should I help you with this?"

McCarthy had reduced the ice ball down to a core which refused to respond to his prying. Henry slipped the ball into a plastic bag he found on top of the freezer, raised the package above his head, and brought it down with both hands, clattering onto the table top a bit closer to McCarthy than was necessary.

"There you are. Chipped ice for your cup of cold water."

The other guests arrived. McCarthy put on his "happy host" face and introductions were made over hors d'oeuvres. Tena Ballard was a tall, strikingly beautiful woman in her late thirties, and approximately seven months' pregnant. Her husband, Jeffry, was a thin man, dark complected, with a receding hairline and delicate features. Had Henry seen them in an international airport, and without the protruding tummy, he would have thought she was a highly paid model, traveling with her personal hairdresser to some exotic shooting location.

Tonight, though, there was a somber air about the two of them. Although they responded politely to the McCarthys' efforts at light conversation, they volunteered very little of themselves. No doubt they viewed the dinner as an obligation, and would be relieved to have it over and done with.

"Henry's an old friend of mine," McCarthy explained.

"Here to do a little work for me at the Center."

The comment didn't seem to perk anyone's curiosity, for the only response was a smile and a nod from Professor Ballard in Henry's general direction. The hors d'oeuvres tray was passed around again, primarily to fill in a gap in the conversation.

Then McCarthy's bubbling voice cracked the silence: "Henry, I think you'll find Professor Ballard's work of great interest."

"Oh, yes, I'm most anxious!" Mrs. McCarthy chimed in.

"He's working on a contraceptive device—or method that interrupts the genetic mixture of the cells—the male and female cells—from meshing. Did I explain that right, Jeffry?"

"Yes, that's the general idea," Ballard agreed, reluctantly.

"Sounds interesting," Henry urged.

"We're pretty close to an announcement on that, aren't we?" asked McCarthy.

"Oh, no, no. We've had some partial successes with lower animals, but we have a long way to go."

Henry couldn't be sure, but he thought Mrs. Ballard's act of tugging at her evening jacket to slightly cover her pregnancy related somehow to her husband's comment that they had a "long way to go."

"But I thought . . . Dr. Robinson gave me to understand we were close to an announcement."

"Dr. Robinson is premature."

McCarthy was genuinely disappointed. "But things are looking promising?"

"Yes, of course."

"Oh, I think it's so fascinating," Millie McCarthy bubbled, "to be in on the planning, the ground floor so to speak, of something so important! But tell me, how does it work? Vern mentioned something about viruses."

"Yes, viruses," Ballard cleared his throat and went on, "we're discovering, can have a strong influence on the genetic code and we're developing a virus strain that will change certain elements . . . or camouflage certain elements in the code, so the sperm and the egg will think they are from different species and will not join."

"Oh, good heavens," Millie exclaimed. "You mean people will have to go out and catch a cold before they can . . . oh, good heavens!" She shrieked with laughter.

Jeffry Ballard frowned. "There are many kinds of viruses, Mrs. McCarthy."

"I imagine this kind of research would be quite expensive, wouldn't it?" Henry asked as casually as he could.

"Time consuming. It's expensive in that sense. Fortunately, the Langtree Family Planning Foundation is underwriting the entire cost."

"Oh, I see."

"Marvelous, isn't it?" McCarthy mused. "This genetic management business. Man is truly on the verge of controlling his own destiny."

"Yes, it is," Jeffry answered, as his face brightened. "I've been working so closely, for so long, on the subject, perhaps I can't see the forest for the trees. But I do feel it's going to change man."

"It's going to be man's salvation!" McCarthy declared.

"Oh, I don't know about that," Ballard smiled.

"I've heard Thomas Edison was asked what the primary use would be for his invention, the phonograph. You know what his reply was?" Henry asked.

After a pause Mrs. McCarthy asked the question: "No, what did he say?"

"He said he thought the primary use of the phonograph would be to record last wills and testaments."

"What is that supposed to mean?" McCarthy asked bluntly.

"It means," Ballard interceded for Henry, "it means, if a genius like Edison couldn't foresee the record industry, who are we to presume to know the future?"

Henry nodded agreement and Ballard continued.

"You have a point—Pandora's box and all that. But have you considered the alternative? Suppose we don't act. Have you really considered that, with all its ramifications?"

Before Henry could respond, the kitchen door opened with a bang and in raced the boy from the garage. Mrs. McCarthy demonstrated a surprising agility in corraling the boy and marching him before the guests for his formal introduction. He was Vernon Dennis Jr., seven and a half years old, and he was going to be a race-car driver when he grew up.

After his mother calmly and carefully introduced each guest to Vernon Dennis Jr., the boy said, "Good-bye, all you dumb dopes," giggled and tried to squirm out of his mother's grasp.

The McCarthys were mortified, especially Mrs. McCarthy, who apologized profusely and tried to get a retraction from her son.

Without saying a word, Mrs. Ballard rose and knelt before the boy. Taking his busy little hands in hers, she looked at him for a moment then hugged him. The boy could take about a second of this before he squirmed away.

"You don't mind if I hug you, do you?"

"I don't like that," the boy announced and was led away to have his dinner in another part of the house.

McCarthy explained his son had a hyperactive condition that seemed to have been aggravated by the move west. While he went on at some length about his son's problems, Henry noticed Jeffry Ballard reach over and give his wife's hand a private little squeeze. Tena Ballard was fighting back tears.

Dinner was a production. Vern McCarthy was the director, Mrs. M. and the maid were the stagehands, and Henry and the Ballards were the audience. There was much to-do made when the maid missed her cue in removing the pewter plates, and Mrs. M. had to be reminded the chilled forks were served after, not before, the salad arrived. This last fine point Mrs. M. objected to, she said, because she always felt some guests might start using their dinner forks and she would like to save them the embarrassment by serving the salad forks first. However, she did as her husband asked.

Henry smiled and went along. His was a very flat palate and, except as nourishment and an excuse for good conversation, food held little interest for him, much less how it was served. The dinner protocol only acted to make him nervous.

Finally, when they were well into the main course, things

quieted down and the conversation hopped from one safe topic to another, until Jeffry Ballard announced, "I have a question for you, Mr. Garrott."

"Very well."

"If all the food in the world were divided equally among all the peoples of the world, what do you suppose our daily allotment would be?"

"I'm sure it would be something less than what we are enjoying this evening."

"To say the least. Our daily share would be slightly less than the nourishment found in one eight-ounce glass of milk." Ballard's lips thinned and he measured his words carefully. "Can you imagine functioning all day on that? And in the future, it's going to be worse, not better. When the oil depletion occurs—when, not if—our agricultural industries, which depend so heavily on mechanization and petroleum-based fertilizers, will be helpless.

"We will have a situation, Mr. Garrott, somewhat reminiscent of the black plagues of the Middle Ages."

"Heavens!" Mrs. McCarthy gasped.

"You paint a very bleak picture," Henry remarked, while cutting his asparagus. "I suppose your purpose in telling us all this is to justify your research project."

"Why, of course," Ballard countered, with a surprised laugh. "It's only reasonable."

"Reasonable . . . " Henry measured the word with a tinge of disdain. "I've heard the third world is beginning to control its population gro—"

"That's wishful thinking by the rich nations," Ballard scoffed.

"And on the other hand, who are we to deny the poor man a large family? In many emerging countries a large family is social security—the only assurance a parent has that one or two children will be alive to take care of him in his old age."

"Who said anything about forced sterilization?" Ballard retorted.

"No one has, yet. I'm no scientist, but I do know viruses can be very hard to control."

"You don't know what you're talking about."

"Jeffry!" Tena Ballard scowled.

"Perhaps you're right," Henry conceded. "I suppose the point I'm trying to make is this: I've had several years of close-hand experience observing and participating in 'grand designs'—the elite few spreading goodness to the masses through their superior intellect." Henry shook his head. "From where I sit, it does not work."

Ballard sneered, "Surely you're not suggesting the intelligent people of a nation should be denied positions of leadership?"

"The question is, what *kind* of leadership? I think individuals generally look after their own welfare pretty well."

McCarthy piped in, "You realize, Henry, you are flying directly into the face of . . . completely contrary to the philosophy of the Center."

"I hadn't thought about that."

"All right," Ballard offered, warming to the subject, "let's suppose you *are* right. If the ivory tower system has failed, why do you suppose it has?"

"Well, perhaps man is not as smart as he thinks he is . . . or perhaps men's motives are not quite as pure as they would have us believe they are. There's a marvelous line in the Old Testament—when the ancient Hebrews started to slip away from faith the writer said, 'In those days . . . every man did that which was right in his own eyes.' "

"What's wrong with that?" Ballard shrugged.

"Yes, what indeed?" Henry said.

"What does man have but his own intellect, his own sense of rightness?" Ballard asked.

"I think you should know," McCarthy said with a sly smile, "that Henry here is a recent convert to Christianity."

"Oh, brother!" Ballard sighed with disgust.

"Perhaps he would like to return us to the days of the Spanish Armada and the Crusades—speaking of 'grand Designs.' " McCarthy laughed.

From the way Ballard was concentrating on his dinner, Henry felt the conversation was at an end, but he had a genuine curiosity about the attitude of first-order scientists toward religion. He couldn't help asking, "Now let me ask a question,

Mr. Ballard. Do you believe in God?"

Cutting his meat, Ballard answered, "I am not concerned with such questions. I'm a scientist."

"That's a cop-out," Henry declared flatly, startling even himself. "You are a human being with an excellent mind, on the threshold of a profound discovery—a discovery which you claim will have far-reaching ramifications. We have a right to know upon what ethical basis you make your value judgments."

Ballard carefully laid down his knife and fork and looked Henry in the eye. "Mr. Garrott, the universe is barren, dark and void with only occasional spots of unimaginable violence. In this one little patch where we find life to exist, it is an existence without reason or meaning. We are forced into a life we did not choose, filled with disappointment and pain. We sustain ourselves only by preying on other life." He held up his fork with a piece of rare beef on it; his voice brittle, he continued, "And it is over, not with conclusion or fulfillment, but with heartache and . . . I choose to believe there is no God, Mr. Garrott, for if there is a God, he must surely be the most sadistic, evil villain imaginable. Such a thought I could not bear."

By the time Ballard finished, his hand was trembling, his wife sobbed quietly without wiping her eyes, while Henry studied the patterns in the tablecloth, wishing to heaven he'd kept his mouth shut.

After what seemed an eternity, Mrs. McCarthy held the small silver carafe aloft and said brightly, "Would anyone care for more of the sauce?"

Back in his motel room, while undressing, Henry couldn't help replaying the evening's events in his mind. A smile crossed his face as he thought of all the polite platitudes and clichés that were exchanged after Ballard's speech. How strange it was in our society, that to speak of one's inner fears and heart's convictions was somehow always embarrassing. That should not be. He wondered what was creating all the sadness in the Ballards' lives. They were very attractive people, and he wanted to take them both in his arms and hold them close until all their cares were swept away.

Good grief! Where did such a thought come from? He must be getting ready for grandparenthood.

Henry had amazed himself. He had feared his new-found faith would crumble at the first onslaught of the world's arrows; that somehow he had to buttress it from within before he was ready for a confrontation. Now that it had happened, he found his faith more solid than ever. No doubt the anguish and hurt he could see in Ballard's eyes had influenced him more than Ballard's words. Was it right to say—yes. It made him feel happy. Henry sang to himself,

"Because He lives,
I can face tomorrow;
Because He lives,
All fear is gone. . . . "*

He turned on the air conditioner to drown out the traffic noise from outside, then climbed into bed. He wished he were home. Why had he agreed to come up here on a Friday? Now he was stuck with a weekend and nothing to do that couldn't be done at home. He definitely would go home in the a.m., he decided, so he set his alarm accordingly.

As he closed his eyes, another thought of the evening's dinner crossed his mind and Henry actually chuckled out loud: How could McCarthy and his people hope to control the world when he couldn't even control his own son?

Saturday

Henry stood on the gravel observation area where he and McCarthy had stopped Friday morning to look at the

---

*From "Because He Lives," by William J. and Gloria Gaither. © 1971 by William J. Gaither. Used by permission.

Center—except now he was alone, and the Center which should have been on a distant hill was suddenly moving down the hillside toward the ravine separating the hills. As it moved, it was drawing with it the scrub oak and underbrush from the surrounding area. At first the observation area seemed secure, but soon small chunks of the hillside began to give way and were sucked into the vibrant, growing Center.

As larger and larger chunks were drawn off the hillside, Henry found he couldn't move his legs. The guard rail appeared quite strong and secure, so he reached over and gripped the steel railing. But the relentless sucking action, coming from the Center, weakened one post, and then another, until the railing itself started buckling and hanging over the edge. Henry looked down and saw the ravine getting deeper and deeper.

The old station wagon was still parked on the other side of the observation area, and he called out, hoping there was someone inside who would hear his cry for help. The windows were all splattered with mud, and he had no way of knowing whether or not he was being heard.

Finally, the back door opened, and a ramp was slowly let down onto the ground. In slow motion Henry was beginning to hang farther over into the ravine.

The loud revving of motorcycles sounded, and three boys on plastic Big Wheels came charging out of the station wagon toward Henry. As they drew near, he could see the first boy was Vernon Dennis Jr., and his two friends were the little cartoon characters from the old Katzenjammer cartoons. They all screeched and whirled about, having a grand time.

Henry kept calling to them, trying to be heard over the din of the motorcycle noises. He braced his left arm up on the road bed and gave one last shout. They spotted him and raced over, but instead of getting off their vehicles to help, they began taking turns running over Henry's left arm. The arm started swelling to about three times its normal size and Henry wondered why the rythmical bumping of the tires didn't hurt him more than it did.

He awoke and found he was gripping the sideboard of his

bed. All the frightful elements of his dream faded quickly—
except for the throbbing in his arm. Sitting up to examine himself, he found the back of his left wrist was swollen, and, he
thought, slightly discolored. He removed the bandage from the
palm of his hand but found no trace of an infection around the
small wound.

The throbbing frightened him, and he felt feverish. He
glanced at the clock—6:20; stuck in a strange town with no
doctor. He found the phone directory and dialed Dr. Robinson's home number. To his surprise, Robinson answered after
just one ring, and he sounded wide awake. Henry apologized
for the hour and proceeded to give him his symptoms.

"See, I told you there was something in there."

"The question is, now what do I do about it? I don't know
a soul in this town," Henry said.

"Okay, do you think you can drive?"

"Oh, sure."

"Then, why don't I meet you at the Center?"

"I hate to put you out like this."

"No problem, no problem at all. I'm on my way up there
anyway."

"At this hour?" Henry asked.

"Yes, we've got some problems to work out, and this seems
to be the only time to do it. I've got a whole refrigerator full of
antibiotics here. I'll bring something along. You're not allergic
to penicillin are you?"

"No."

"Okay. The first thing to do is get that infection under control, then we'll go from there. I'll probably get there first so
just come around to the north door of the Great Hall and
knock. I'll let you in."

The confidence Robinson exuded seemed to make Henry
feel better. He dressed and drove out to the Center without any
problem, and circled around to the parking lot on the north
side.

The sun was just coming over the eastern hills, and Henry
stopped for a moment to enjoy the sight and to feel the welcome warmth. He leaned against the car door and thought of

the song his Bible study group had sung: "Good morning, Lord. It's great to see the sun again. . . . "*

As he came up the steps he could hear voices in the Great Hall. He thought they were male voices, but because of the echo, and his own lack of concentration, he could not say for sure. He knocked on the double doors with his good hand and waited. The voices continued. It sounded as though people were on the scaffold arguing, as he had seen Robinson and Shoemaker doing the day before. He was about to rap again when he heard a loud cry. Immediately, there was the sound of breaking plastic and clanging steel, then someone crying out in pain.

Henry yelled, "Dr. Robinson? Dr. Robinson?" and began kicking the door. When this brought no immediate response he pressed his ear to the crack between the doors. He heard someone climbing down the scaffold, then nothing except the moaning from the person who must have fallen. Henry pounded again. No one answered. He searched in the landscaping nearby for a stone large enough to smash the narrow translucent window inset in the door. Since it was wire-reinforced, it took longer than expected to smash enough glass away so he could reach in and release the door lock from the inside.

He rushed into the main hall; Robinson was lying in a mass of broken wires and smashed plastic from the double helix. He lay grotesquely on his back, one leg twisted under him and his chest elevated some six inches off the ground. No one else was in sight.

The sudden silence in the Great Hall gave Henry the uncomfortable feeling he had experienced the morning before, but now intensified. He stood frozen for a moment, half expecting someone else to rush to Robinson's aid. But there was no one else—at least no one else who was going to help.

Henry kicked his way through the broken plastic and other debris to the foot of the scaffold where Robinson lay. There was a sharp protrusion under the front of Robinson's smock.

Henry opened the smock and discovered a half-inch steel brace had punctured Robinson's back when he fell, and he was lying impaled on it. This was what was keeping his chest elevated. It appeared to have pierced the left lung.

Robinson was groaning in a semi-conscious state, but when Henry tried to move him onto his side, he woke up with a cry.

"I'm Garrott, Dr. Robinson. Can you—"

Robinson grabbed Henry by the lapel with his right hand and stared at him, his eyes filled with terror. Frightened, Henry recoiled from what he saw.

"You've fallen from the scaffold—you've had a bad fall," Henry said, but he didn't seem to be getting through. Robinson continued to stare wildly at him. "Can you lie over on your side?"

Robinson coughed blood weakly, then gurgled, "Don't let 'um kill us—"

"Kill us? Who's trying to kill us?"

Robinson shook his head rapidly. Henry couldn't tell if he was disagreeing with him or trying to clear his throat. Robinson tried to speak again but couldn't. He pointed to his own forehead and then to the scaffold area above him.

"What is it? What do you mean? Were you pushed? Who's trying to kill us?"

Robinson shook his head slowly now as though he were giving up. His eyes rolled up behind his lids and he coughed again.

Attempting to prevent the blood flow from getting into his good lung and to clear his breathing, Henry rolled him onto his left side. Robinson must have passed out, for this time he offered no resistance. Henry pushed his fingers down his throat and cleared the obstruction as best he could. He was still breathing, so he decided to leave well enough alone while he searched for a phone. There was one, of course, in McCarthy's office but the locked door looked much too formidable. As he headed toward the Supply Room area, he heard the revving of a big car engine on the south side of the building.

Henry raced to the south side of the Great Hall and vaulted

onto the top of a table. By jumping up and down like a jack-in-the-box, he got a glimpse through the skylight, of the top of the car as it raced by. It had a distinctive black Landau top over the back portion of the white roof—just like Shoemaker's big Oldsmobile.

After two attempts at jimmying doors and breaking more glass, Henry found a phone that worked. He called emergency services and ordered an ambulance. When the operator asked if he wanted the police notified, without thinking, he replied, "Yes."

He then dialed McCarthy's home number and got a sleepy response from Millie. Vern was on a jogging program, and Saturday morning was his time to run. She would give him Henry's message about the accident, and was sure he would come right over. Henry urged her to take the car and search for him.

As he rose to return to the Great Hall, Henry felt very lightheaded. This was the first time he remembered about his own condition and why he had come. Had someone lured Robinson out here assuming they would be alone, to murder him? If only he had come a minute earlier.

Back in the hall, Henry sat helplessly by as Robinson's breathing grew steadily weaker. Taking his own sweater off, he put it over Robinson's back, trying to keep him warm and comfortable. Robinson's left hand was jammed under him and Henry pulled it free so Robinson was now lying three-quarters on his face.

Henry spotted a small patch of material in Robinson's left hand. It appeared to be a pocket made of the same material as his smock. Since Robinson's pockets were all intact Henry assumed that as Robinson fell, or was pushed, he had reached for that other person and ripped the breast pocket off the person's smock.

It seemed like an eternity—but it was only eleven minutes by his watch—before he heard the welcome sound of sirens weaving up the hill and into the north parking lot.

Before the ambulance attendants arrived, McCarthy came

rushing in, wearing a sweat-soaked running suit.

"Oh, no! What happened?"

Henry started to reply, then McCarthy went on.

"There's a police car out there. You didn't call the police, did you?"

"Yes, I did."

"You fool, you! You fool!" McCarthy gasped.

Just then the ambulance attendants entered on the run.

Henry stood up quickly to give them directions, and immediately passed out.

When he woke up, his head was exploding with pain, and someone's movements were jostling him about. It took him several seconds to realize he was in a fast-moving ambulance and two attendants were frantically working on Dr. Robinson on the cot next to him. Their actions and comments indicated their efforts were proving futile.

In the emergency ward of the county hospital, Henry sat in a small examining area while a team of medical people labored over Robinson on the other side of a curtain. McCarthy and his wife arrived. Henry could see them pacing back and forth in the area outside. He hoped they wouldn't see him, but McCarthy did and came in.

"What happened? What on earth happened?"

In a quiet voice, Henry tried to recount the events from 6:20 on, while at the same time keeping an ear cocked toward the next enclosure.

Before he could finish answering all of McCarthy's nervous questions, a police officer entered, and Henry had to start all over again. When the officer zeroed in on the statement of Robinson's, "Don't let 'um kill us," McCarthy stood helplessly cringing in the corner. He could see his career dissolving before his closed eyes.

When Henry got to the part of seeing the car race away, the officer recorded the information quickly and left.

"No one is supposed to be at the Center on weekends unless we know about it. There's heating and janitorial service." McCarthy went on.

Henry asked, "Does Robinson have a family?"

McCarthy's face fell. "He has a wife."

"She should be notified."

"Yes, of course," McCarthy said flatly. "In the foreign embassies I could just send a telegram," he mumbled as he left.

Things were quiet behind the curtain; they must have taken him away to surgery. Henry lay shivering and perspiring for another half hour before he was attended to. He didn't know what had happened to his sweater.

A young doctor with a blood-spattered gown came in and looked at Henry's wrist. Dr. Robinson was dead, he said offhandedly.

"We couldn't understand why. He hadn't lost that much blood, he was in good health, but his blood count was down, no oxygen. Then we found that a small piece of posterior rib bone had broken loose from that steel shaft puncture and lodged against his heart so one of the valves stayed open. By the time we spotted that, it was too late."

Henry was wheeled to X ray, a piece of foreign matter was found, minor surgery performed, and the doctor presented him with a half inch triangular sliver of orange plastic.

They thought it best to keep Henry in the hospital until his temperature was under control. As he was wheeled into a private room, he found two police officers waiting for him. The one he had spoken to earlier stood silently by as his sergeant did the questioning.

Henry related his story for the third time, without interruption, until he got to the part about seeing the car.

"Are you sure it was Professor Shoemaker's car?"

"No, I'm not. I could only see the roof. But it did look like the roof of his Oldsmobile I rode in yesterday."

"How can you be so sure? There are lots of cars with Landau roofs."

"But there's a distinctive crest on the back panel of an Olds 98."

"And you saw that crest?" he asked, making a note of this.

"Yes. I'm something of a car buff. I saw it."

The sergeant looked at his partner. "I guess that does it."

"What do you mean?" Henry asked.

"We found this Shoemaker, a big hefty guy, walking along a road going away from the Kilbourne Center. He piled his car up on a hillside trying to take a corner too fast."

"You've arrested him?"

"Not yet," the Sergeant said, then held up his notebook, "but we probably will now."

They must have given Henry something to make him sleep along with the antibiotics because the officers were barely out the door when he dozed off.

When he awoke, he found himself staring directly into the eyes of Vern McCarthy.

"What time is it?"

"Four-fifteen," McCarthy said, without looking at his watch.

"Still Saturday?"

"Of course. Man, you sure can sleep."

"What's happened? Did you get ahold of Dr. Robinson's wife?"

McCarthy opened the blind and answered, "Yes, I did."

"How'd she take it?"

"Stoically, I'd say. She said, 'I knew something bad was bound to happen.' "

"Those were her exact words?"

"I think so . . . Yes."

"Why would she say a thing like that?"

"Haven't the foggiest."

"Poor thing. Did she break down?"

"Not while we were there. She didn't even want to come to the hospital. Millie offered to stay with her but she didn't want her to."

"Poor thing."

"Look, we've got real problems, Stop worrying about her, will you?"

"What problems?" Henry asked. "Seems to me this solves one of your biggest problems."

"What do you mean?"

"Your thorn in the side, A. K. Shoemaker. Here he's been giving you fits with his 'Low-I.Q.'s-for-Blacks' lectures around the country. Now he gets into an argument with a black and accidentally kills him and then runs away. The man's . . . " He didn't finish.

"What's the matter?" McCarthy asked.

"I don't know. Somehow the whole thing doesn't gel."

"Why doesn't it? It sounds good to me. I hadn't even thought of that angle. *If* we can only weather this publicity storm. Why, oh why, did we have to have that big grant pending now? I'm going to have a nervous breakdown!"

"Have you talked with Shoemaker?"

"No. I don't plan to, either."

"Maybe we should get his version of all this."

"Leave it alone, man; leave it alone."

A nurse whisked in, took Henry's pulse and temperature, and pronounced him fit to leave after he had something to eat. As she left, McCarthy rose as if he were leaving, too.

"Where are you going?"

McCarthy looked preoccupied. "I just came by to make sure you were getting along okay."

"Can you stick around? I'll need a ride out to get my car."

"Oh, I drove it down for you. It's out in front," McCarthy said, tossing the keys onto the bed.

"Did the police find the smock?"

"Smock?"

"The smock with the torn pocket. Did they find it?"

"What are you talking about?"

"In Robinson's left hand, I found a pocket ripped off a lab coat. I thought the police would be searching for that coat," Henry said.

"Oh, I don't know."

"You remember . . . when was it? Yesterday morning when we came to the Center and Shoemaker and Robinson were on the scaffold arguing. What was that all about?"

"I don't know."

Henry studied McCarthy. He had the feeling McCarthy was being evasive. "You're a real bundle of information, aren't you?"

"Look, what's the point in pursuing this? It's in the hands of the police now."

"You're the director of this place. Don't you know what your people are up to?"

McCarthy sat down again. "Robinson had an independent research grant to work on sickle-cell anemia. He had a theory that the secret to its control, and eventual elimination, lay in the manipulation of the genetic code. He invited himself out here to work with our genetic team; we thought it would be good for the record to have a black on the staff, and he was welcomed with open arms. As far as I know, the argument yesterday was the first indication of any disagreement, although a couple of weeks ago Miss Matthews did say he was upset about something."

"How long had he been at the Center?"

"About seven months. Look—"

Henry interrupted. "Why was he on the Finance Committee?"

"What?"

"Robinson was on the Finance Committee. His name was even on the signature card for the General Operating Fund."

"That was Begelman's idea. He was a big booster of Robinson's. Thought the sun rose and set on him."

"Begelman—"

"Look, why are you concerning yourself with all this? Let the police handle it."

"Fine. I was just trying to pursue the possibility of a connection between Robinson's death and the missing funds."

"Oh." A light went on in the back of McCarthy's head. His eyes darted about the room, first to Henry, then the window and back again.

This man should never play poker, thought Henry.

"Shoemaker's name was on the card, too," Henry added.

"Ye-es . . . you're right."

McCarthy excused himself, explaining he had to get home and work on a press release regarding Dr. Robinson's death.

Henry dressed and ate the light meal a nurse's aide brought in. His wrist was stiff and painful, now that the local anesthetic had worn off, and he was surprised to see how dependent he was on his left hand for normal, daily functions.

McCarthy's attitude disturbed Henry again. He had come into his room to talk about their "real problems," then made no further mention of it after he had second thoughts about Shoemaker's troubles. This sense of mistrust was the reason he didn't explain to McCarthy why the Shoemaker theory didn't gel. When Henry had pressed his ear to the outside door at the Center, he had heard someone coming down the scaffold steps, but it wasn't the squeaky rattling sound a man of Shoemaker's weight would make. It wasn't as loud as the noises he had heard the day before when Shoemaker and Robinson came down the same scaffold.

Then again, perhaps he simply couldn't hear all that well from the distance of the north entrance . . . and no doubt the person was trying to be as quiet as possible. But, then again, he was in a hurry. This could go on forever. Perhaps he didn't know what he heard. The whole thing started to blur in his memory.

Back in his motel room, Henry was about to call his wife and was startled when the phone rang just as he grabbed the receiver. It was A. K. Shoemaker.

Apparently he had not been arrested; he asked Henry if he would come over to his apartment for a talk. Henry expressed reluctance to do so, but finally agreed to have a cup of coffee with him in a small restaurant near his apartment.

Henry found the grubby little cafe with no problem, and spotted Shoemaker standing by the back booth waving to him. The man looked a mess. He had a small bandage over the bridge of his nose, and his lower lip was split and swollen. Obviously, he had not cleaned up or changed his suit since the accident early that morning. Judging from the ash tray with seven butts in it, he'd been chain-smoking since he'd arrived.

"What can I get you? You want something to eat?"

"Just coffee is fine," Henry said, sliding in opposite Shoemaker.

"You want some pie? They have very good pie here."

"No, the coffee is fine."

They ordered two coffees—then Shoemaker studied his cup without speaking.

Henry began: "I suppose you heard I saw your car leaving the Center this morning?"

He nodded yes. "It was me, all right."

"You were with Robinson on the scaffold?"

"No, I didn't know anyone else was out there. I was in my office last night, working late. I meant to take a nap and get up and work some more, but I slept right through. Very unusual for me. I didn't wake up until I heard someone running down the hall in the office wing."

"You didn't hear the DNA model smashing to the floor?"

He shook his head.

"It made quite a racket."

"My office is clear down the east wing. I can't hear anything from there."

Henry was trying to look into Shoemaker's eyes, but they kept darting about, except for occasional quick glances at Henry. He seemed to look younger. Henry had estimated his age in the mid-fifties Friday morning, but now, with his self-assurance gone, the voice patterns and gestures were those of a much younger man. He rattled off his excuses so glibly it was almost as though he had been rehearsing.

"It's terrible—terrible about Robinson, but think what this is doing to *my* career! I'm an innocent bystander. I had nothing to do with it. I'm a scientist. I do scientific research and I report my findings without bias. I don't get involved. I've always treated Robinson with respect and dignity. Don't you see that?" His voice was rising.

"Professor Shoemaker, why are you telling me this? I told the police the truth, and you have just verified it. You did drive away from the Center early this morning and at a very fast speed."

He scowled almost as though he'd been struck, then stirred his coffee. "I don't know why I'm telling you.

"Oh, God, I can see it now. I can just see the future. I'll spend the rest of my life buttonholing people in little restaurants, telling them I didn't do it—anyone who will listen. Don't you see? Robinson was the last person in the world I'd pick a fight with. I gotta treat all blacks with kid gloves, otherwise all my data will be immediately suspect. He's the last person in the world—" He stopped, realizing he was starting to repeat himself, shook his head in frustration and rubbed his forehead.

Henry probed, "Friday morning, when I came into the hall with Mr. McCarthy, you were on the scaffold arguing with Dr. Robinson. What was that all about?"

"Arguing! We weren't arguing."

"All right, you were having a heated discussion—about what?"

"It's very complicated. How can I explain this? Recently we've developed the ability to break into the genetic structure and literally change it. The possibilities are fantastic. It's going to be a whole new science.

"For instance, we'll be able to take undesirable insects and induce them to breed themselves out of existence after approximately ten generations. A team back east is developing a strain of mice which is highly resistant to cancer. We can now bypass several generations of plant breeding to improve the species of, say, wheat, that will resist black stem rust by joining the most desirable traits of two existing plant genes.

"I could go on and on. Needless to say, we are only in the horse-and-buggy stage right now. Working with these codes is something like trying to thread a needle with a scoop shovel. We're still learning which elements of the code control which traits. It's extremely complicated.

"Anyway, Robinson and I were arg . . . discussing which elements fit into our model at a particular point. I don't mean to run Robinson down. I'm sure he's a good M.D., an excellent M.D. But he's just not a research scientist. Ever since he came to the Center, he's been sticking his nose into everything, expecting to be taught. We don't have time to stop and teach. He should go back to school if he wants to learn basics."

"You speak as though he were still alive. You do know he died, don't you?"

"Yes. The police were kind enough to inform me. I don't know why I do that. I guess I just don't want him to be dead. I tried to help him. He was very interested in those elements of the code which control pigmentation in humans. That's my specialty. Because of my work with the relationships between intelligence and pigmentation, I suppose I'm the foremost authority in the area. He wanted to argue. The man was grossly misinformed by somebody, and he wouldn't let me continue my work on the model."

"And that's what you were talking about yesterday?"

"Yes."

"Who decides how that model is shaped?"

"I'm in charge of that particular section. We all—everyone on the genetic team—have our special areas."

"So he couldn't really have restricted your work indefinitely?"

"No, no way," Shoemaker answered.

"I see. Hardly a motivation to push him off the platform, is it?" Henry mused.

"Exactly!" Shoemaker cried, grasping the signal. "I had no motivation at all. In fact, my entire motivation, my entire desire would be to keep him alive, to keep him alive—"

Shoemaker's stomach started jiggling as though he were chuckling, but then Henry realized he was crying, but without tears. Shoemaker caught a big breath, then tapped the table for emphasis, as he said, "I've got to find out who was out in that hall!"

"Do you have any idea who it might have been?"

"No. I can't believe it was anyone on staff. It must have been someone from outside—a transient or some kid trying to rob him. The Center is so isolated it could have been anyone."

"At 6:30 in the morning? No. He told me over the phone he was meeting someone there."

"But who? Didn't he say anything that would give you a hint? Anything?"

Henry closed his eyes to better recall the conversation. "He said someting about problems, and this was the only time they could work on them."

"The only time . . . " Shoemaker scratched his head. "I don't understand that. He had plenty of time."

"But maybe the other person was very busy . . . or the other person used it as an excuse to lure Robinson to the Center when no one else would be around."

"You mean . . . you mean you think it was deliberate? It was all planned? But that makes it murder."

"It would, wouldn't it? Premeditated."

Shoemaker blinked thoughtfully and brushed back the mass of curls from his forehead. "Will you help me? Will you work on this angle? I don't have anyone."

"You better get yourself a good lawyer."

"But what about you? Aren't you an investigator of sorts?"

Henry smiled, "I'm investigating another matter, which may or may not be related. If I do uncover anything that would be helpful, I'll certainly let you—"

"Yes, please; please do. Somehow I just knew I could rely on you. I think that's really why I called you. Your Christian background and all."

Henry bristled at the mention of his "Christian background." Here, just one day ago, Shoemaker was dismissing Christianity as an unnecessary appendage to modern life, and now at the first sign of personal trouble, this blubbering slob of a man was appealing to Henry's "Christianity."

Henry had no sooner thought this than he realized how wrong it was. Shoemaker's conceited manner made him an easy man to dislike. Henry even found himself enjoying the sight of Shoemaker turned into a fearful bowl of pudding. But he was a child of God. Christ had died for the sins of A. K. Shoemaker just as he had for Henry Garrott's.

Shoemaker continued on about the importance of his career and the years of valuable research that now stood in jeopardy—when he stopped abruptly, gripped the edge of the table, and looked over Henry's shoulder.

Henry heard the approach of two men with heavy-soled shoes.

"Hello, Lieutenant," Shoemaker said flatly.

"I'm afraid we have some bad news, Professor," said the heavyset man, showing a folded paper to Shoemaker. "We have a warrant for your arrest. Would you like me to read you your rights?"

"No, that won't be necessary," Shoemaker said calmly.

"Okay, let's go."

"But wait—what happened? You guys just let me go an hour ago. I haven't left town or anything."

"We found the smock."

"Smock? What smock?"

"The lab coat you wear at the Center. The one with the missing pocket you tried to hide in the bottom of your four-drawer file."

Shoemaker looked at Henry. "But I always hang my lab coat on the hook behind my door." He turned to the officers, "What lab coat are you talking about?"

The second officer stepped toward Shoemaker. "Look, we're not going to stand here talking about it. Are you going to come along quietly or not?"

Shoemaker slid his huge frame to the edge of the booth, heaved himself to a standing position, and walked toward the exit with the police officers. Henry tried to follow them out, but the man behind the counter called, "Hey, who's paying for the two coffees?"

Waiting for his change, Henry watched the flashing lights on the squad car as it disappeared around a corner.

"Oh, Henry, I do wish you were coming home tomorrow," Valery begged disappointedly. "Rebecca's plans have all been changed. She's coming in to International Airport tomorrow night, and you know how I feel about the freeways."

"What happened to Europe?"

"It's cancelled. The whole tour was cancelled."

"Can they do that?"

"Yes. It's something to do with the change in the exchange rate. The poor dear sounded brokenhearted over the phone."

"Well," Henry drawled, "we'll save a few bucks this way."

"I know, but Aunt Evy was so looking forward to seeing her and showing her about. Don't you want her to know our England?"

"Tell you what. You fix her one of Aunt Evy's kidney pies and feed it to her while I hold the garden hose on the window outside. That'll—"

"That's not funny, Henry."

"Dear, of course not. I've never said Aunt Evy's kidney pies were funny."

"What a thing to say! Is this part of the new-found Christian spirit you talk about?"

"Valery, my spirit is born again, but my taste buds remain adamantly fixed—praise the Lord."

After a long pause Valery asked, "Henry, are you all right?"

"Yes, fine. My back hurts. I've just gotten over a 103° fever, and I can't bend my left wrist. Yes, I do feel just fine."

"I think you're overdoing it. You sound light-headed."

"Yes, you're right. I am still mixed up. I cry when I see a beautiful sunrise, and I want to laugh when people tell me sad stories about how terrible life is. But I've decided there's no cure for it. I'm afraid I'm going to be this way from now on. Do you still love me?"

Another pause. "Henry, I don't understand any of this. Why are we talking about Aunt Evy's kidney pies? Henry, you're fifty-two years old. This is no way to talk. People could be listening in."

He laughed. "All right. If you don't want to drive to the airport, have her take a cab."

"Henry, this is Southern California. We're miles away. . . . Do you know how much that would cost?"

"Well, there's got to be a limousine service."

"Oh, never mind, I'll get her."

"Valery, I would come home, but it's quite important that I be here over Sunday. This is getting more complicated than I thought. I really need to be here to see people *away* from the Center, and Sunday seems to be the only time."

"I understand. It's quite all right. We'll manage. Henry, now listen to me. Are you really truly all right? I can come up and get you if you want."

"Valery, really and truly, I feel better than I have in years. I'm sorry if I upset you. Tell Becky hello, and I'll talk with her tomorrow night. Good-night, honey."

"Good-night, dear. You're sleeping all right? You haven't been dreaming again, have you?"

"Not to speak of. Good-night, honey."

"Good-night."

Henry wanted to make one more call before retiring. He looked up Dr. Marion D. Jones in the directory, and dialed.

"Hello."

"Dr. Jones, this is Henry Garrott calling. I'm doing some work at the Center for your administrator, Vernon McCarthy, and I wonder if I might meet briefly with you sometime tomorrow."

"What kind of work might that be, Mr. Garrott?" She had

a very crisp manner of speaking—not unfriendly but strictly business.

"I'm an accountant. I'm helping him with some of the financial structure of the Center. I understand you are on the committee for the management of the General Fund. I'd like to chat with you about that if I may."

After a pause she said, "I have a tee-off time of 9:14 in the morning, and the afternoon is out of the question. I'll be hitting balls on the practice tee at 8 a.m. We could talk then. Would that be satisfactory?"

"Yes, I guess that would be okay. Where will you—"

"Just go south of town, then follow the Riverbed Road east. It's the only course in the area. You can't miss it."

Henry put out the light and lay in bed gazing at the dark grey ceiling. His adrenalin was running, and he was not ready to sleep. He had, he felt, been a big disappointment to his father because he hadn't shared his father's spirited interest in hunting. Now he recalled his father's hunting tales and realized he was experiencing the same feelings his father used to describe. The prospect of the chase was tantalizing. He was thinking of tracking a human being, but he wondered if some of the same principles might apply to both endeavors. When hunting moose, you learn the habits of the moose—where he sleeps and feeds and what he will do when startled or cornered.

Could the same approach hold true while stalking a human? It was strange how this feeling of exhilaration had never come over him when he was with the Agency; maybe it was the challenge of going one-on-one.

He switched on the light and phoned McCarthy.

"What's up? You all right?" McCarthy asked in a husky, sleep-filled voice.

"I'd like to get a look at the personnel records at the Center."

"What? Oh, well, we don't have personnel records as such. We have biographical sketches used for press releases. Would that do?"

"Yes, sounds good."

"Are you onto something?"

"Well, I—"

"Remember, you're working for me. No more calls to the police at weird hours. Okay?"

"Vernon, the man was dying. The police had to be notified under the circumstances."

"What are you onto?" he asked, after a pause.

"I don't know yet. I want to check into the backgrounds of all the people on that signature card."

"I'll see what I can do. Miss Matthews keeps track of that stuff. Maybe I'll ask her to drop by the Center in the morning and run off some copies for you."

"Good. I'd like to chat with her anyway."

McCarthy wasn't sure she would be available on Sunday, but in a few minutes Miss Matthews called to inform Henry she would meet him at the Center at 9 a.m.

Henry spent another half hour, before sleep overtook him, constructing a mental labyrinth with each of the different suspects at his own starting gate. The object was to move each suspect through a series of turns and blind alleys toward the exit at the other end, which was labelled "Prime Suspect." He first played the game assuming there was a connection between Robinson's death and the missing funds. Lipert the banker had access to funds . . . was bitter about the Center but probably did not have access to traveling schedules of signators . . . dead end . . . plus no other obvious connection to the Center. Dead end.

Ballard could be so dedicated to his research he'd become unstable . . . possible tie-in with Robinson because both were on Finance Committee, plus both working on genetic team. But, no need to steal funds for his work. Dead end.

Begelman had to be up in years, plus recuperating from a stroke. Highly unlikely he would have need for $700,000, or risk his prestigious career.

McCarthy certainly wouldn't mind seeing Shoemaker out of the way, but he wouldn't call Henry in for help finding funds—or would he? Hmmm. He was out jogging Saturday morning, and was very sweaty when he reached the Center. Could he have run cross-country over very hilly terrain from the Center to a road near his house where his wife picked him up? He would find out from Millie exactly where she picked him up, and double-check a city map for proximity. Perhaps he knew Shoemaker was in his office. But killing Robinson to get at Shoemaker? No, no. Dead end. No one seemed to have a motive to kill Robinson.

Perhaps it was an accident, perhaps Henry misunderstood Robinson's dying words, "Don't let 'um kill us." After all, he did shake his head when Henry asked who was trying to kill them. And the "um" . . . was it "them," or "him," or something else. He was struggling against the throat blockage.

Then Henry ran through the sequence again, assuming there was no connection between the death and the missing funds. But this way everyone came up slightly suspected of embezzling and no one of murder. Shoemaker was beginning to look more and more like Number One.

Sunday

Henry expected a restless night but slept soundly until he started stirring just before his alarm went off. While still semiconscious, he heard what sounded like someone's hand tap against the door. By the time he came to his senses and spotted the envelope slipped under the door, whoever left it had disappeared.

It was from Shoemaker. The letter was on cheap notepaper, and was printed in a small, careful hand with several words underlined for emphasis.

Dear Mr. Garrott,

Have thought of many things you should know in your search for the culprit who pushed our dear Dr. Robinson. Number one need is *motive*! Find out where *Jeffry Ballard* was Saturday a.m. His obvious motive could have been a deep-seated hatred of blacks. Very sad background. His oldest son died at ten years of age after suffering all his short life from genetic lung disease, cystic fibrosis. Then two weeks to the day, his second son was killed in a school bus accident. Child was being bussed into racially mixed community in Boston area. Blacks were fighting whites in front of bus. Driver backed bus up without looking, crushing Ballard boy. Child died that eve. Was in all eastern papers. That's why Ballard moved out here. Strange fellow. Plays it close-to-vest, but first-class mind.

Dr. Marion Jones. Motive: Bitter about losing bid for money from General Fund. Her good friend and co-researcher B. Corbut *died* in Cleveland the night they got bad news. Although vote was secret, everyone knew Robinson voted issue down! Big research project washed out. Don't remember details. B. Corbut was social scientist, big booster of B. F. Skinner, the behavioral psychologist. Jones' background: advertising. I voted for project. Sounded harmless and cost minimal. Around $175,000 requested, as I recall.

Long-shot suspect: Mrs. Begelman. Husband suffering from stroke after-effects, but can write. Working on big paper. Wife *very protective* and won't let others near Begelman, but Robinson always pestering him for info on DNA code. Challenged some of his pet theories.

Can't think of others.

Good News! Lab coat found in my file was *size medium*! I always wore a *large*. I'm expecting release soon.

Let me know if you hear *anything*!

Sincerely,
A. K. Shoemaker

P.S. Court-appointed lawyer is delivering this. Don't think much of him, but don't know what else to do. Any ideas? Please keep in touch.

Well, if Henry needed motives to think about, this letter helped considerably, however prejudiced the source. He wondered what he had done or said to give Shoemaker the impression he was working for him.

In the lobby he found a local paper which headlined, "Local Researcher Dead from Fall." In the body of the story, the article mentioned Shoemaker was held for questioning, but nothing about an arrest.

Henry reread Shoemaker's letter over a quick breakfast in the coffee shop, trying to formulate an approach he might use in talking with Dr. Jones. He had always felt uneasy talking with a woman as an adversary. He had never been able to get much out of them by questioning, as they always seemed to suspect ulterior motives under the straight questions, and they often misread the purpose of entire interviews. He resolved to be as straightforward and direct as possible.

The early morning coastal fog gradually gave way to sunny skies as he drove inland along the north shores of the riverbed. By the time he reached the Rancho Del Sol Golf Course, it was obviously going to be a great day. The glistening bright green of the fairways contrasted beautifully against the drab grey-brown of the surrounding hills. Man truly could improve upon nature when he put his mind to it.

Marion Jones was a muscular, almost plump, woman in her forties. Judging from the well-worn golf shoes and the colorful but totally practical costume she wore, Henry surmised she took the game quite seriously. They were virtually alone on the driving range, and after introductions, Henry pulled an aluminium lawn chair over so they could talk while she practiced.

After she made a few swings with her five iron, Henry made the mistake of joking about the loop in her backswing.

Her steely glare told him what she thought of kibitzing. "Just loosening up the shoulder, Mr. Garrott," was her reply. "Now, what can I do for you?"

"I understand Bertha Corbut was a good friend of yours."

"That's right. I wouldn't be at the Center if it weren't for her."

"And you were working on a common project?"

"Right again."

"Could you tell me about it?"

"I thought you wanted to talk about finances."

"Yes . . . all right. You and Miss Corbut were both on the

Finance Committee, weren't you?"

"Finance? Oh, you mean the General Fund Adminstration Committee."

"What?" Henry laughed. "This is strange. Every person I talk to has a different title for this group. I get the feeling I'm working with a headless monster."

Dr. Jones let out a hearty laugh that echoed from the quiet morning hills. "Welcome to the club, Mr. Garrott. I can't think of a better description of our committee—of our entire Center for that matter. We're a collection of over-educated prima donnas, all interested in doing our own thing. What we really need are more Indians and fewer chiefs. Nobody wants to get his hands dirty tending to the mundane, such as taking care of books."

"But I understand you volunteered to work on the committee," Henry said. "Why did you do that if you weren't willing to work?"

"Position, Mr. Garrott. Political position. We knew for a long time we were going to be short on our own funds, so we decided early-on to stack that committee as best we could to insure access to that money. Bertha, bless her heart, even volunteered to act as treasurer. She had all she could do to balance her own checkbook."

As she spoke, Dr. Jones was lofting five-iron shots into a neat little pattern around a marker flag, approximately one hundred and fifty yards distant. Each shot seemed to be struck more softly than the last, but the results always seemed the same.

"But all our efforts were for naught," she said, dumping out some more balls from the basket. "We didn't get committee approval."

She made this statement quite matter-of-factly and Henry watched her eyes for a moment to see if there was anything but golfer's concentration to be seen in them. There wasn't.

"I understand Dr. Robinson voted you down."

"He was the most vocal. The only one who was vocal, come to think of it. We did everything we could think of to get approval. We even lined up a P.R. tour of our program in Cleveland. Granted, Cleveland is no Bermuda, but they all came except Dr. Begelman. I thought sure we had it in the bag. But . . . something happened."

"Let's see," Henry figured, "you had a six-member committee, and you needed what for approval? A majority?"

"That's where our problems started. The rules of the committee were designed for a much larger group—twelve, originally—but we couldn't get more to serve, so we were only six. The rules state you have to have a majority, plus one, to have funds approved. That meant, of course, two votes would kill us . . . and it did."

"I see."

"No, I'm wrong on that point. We were a seven-person committee at the time of the critical vote. McCarthy, by virtue of his position, was automatically on the committee. He had just recently arrived. But Dr. Begelman was ill that day, so there were only six votes cast. Yes, that was it."

"And you and Miss Corbut were in Cleveland, I believe."

"Yes."

"How did you vote from there?"

"Professor Ballard carried our proxies."

"Why didn't you call Dr. Begelman and get him to issue his proxy or ask for another vote?"

She chuckled slowly, remembering. "Yes, why . . . all those things went through our minds—after the fact. The vote was timed poorly. The Ad Council had to have its answer the day of the vote. When it was no, the whole project was washed out. They weren't going to support us if we couldn't support ourselves. All we needed was a bit over one hundred thousand dollars. You remember that old poem, 'For want of a nail, the war was lost'? Well that was us. We sat down and cried like a couple of high-school girls stood-up at their first prom."

"What was the nature of your project?"

"So we get around to it after all, don't we? All right. We had worked out an agreement with the National Ad Council, the Department of Health, Education and Welfare, and the Federal Trade Commission, and through them, the Internal Revenue Service—are you still with me?"

Henry nodded.

"Anyway, we arranged a deal with all these agencies to

grant special tax deductions to companies that advertise on national television if they would subject their advertising campaigns to certain requirements our committee would dictate."

"What kind of requirements?"

"Let's go back a bit. You remember the old Clark Gable movie, 'It Happened One Night'? There's a scene in that film where Gable takes off his shirt and he has no undershirt on. Now, because of the attractiveness of the actor, and the wide success of the film, it nearly ruined the undershirt market in this country. It didn't really recover until World War II. If Gable wasn't going to wear an undershirt, the American men weren't going to wear them either.

"The same influences are working on television today. When a woman stands in front of a camera with a bar of soap in hand, she's not just selling soap, but the cut of her clothes, the jewelry, as well as her hair style. And if you show an ad with a domestic scene for an air freshener, you're also selling the manners and morays of that family, along with the air freshener."

"So this was a commercial enterprise to sell subliminally."

"No, no, you misunderstand." For the first time she forgot her golf, took a step toward Henry and faced him directly. "This was very noncommercial—altruistic if you will . . . an honest attempt to influence the life-style of our nation with positive input."

"I'm confused. I'm afraid I don't follow—"

"Let me give you an example. We ran a test program for two years, to see if this concept would work. We took a social problem, and took before-and-after surveys to see if there was any change after our mass-advertising-influence program."

"What social problem did you work on?"

She studied Henry for a moment with her blue-grey eyes. "This is not for publication, I take it?"

"Certainly not," he assured her.

"It's water over the dam now, but I'd just as soon not have it become common knowledge.

"Did you know that fifty percent of our black population is born out of wedlock? And that well over fifty percent of the black children are raised in homes where there is not a constant father figure present?"

Henry didn't know if this was a rhetorical question, or if she was expecting him to respond. Finally he ventured, "Well, I think a lot of that problem can be traced to the policies of the old slave owners, and the blacks' unsettled background."

"Of course. And the current black unemployment factor plays a part. But I think you'll agree it is desirable to have a majority of our future citizens, black or white, coming from stable homes, wouldn't you? I mean, there are all kinds of statistical evidence to indicate that productive, creative citizens are products of stable backgrounds, for the most part."

"I don't think A. K. Shoemaker would agree with that. He says the genes dictate intelligence, and blacks—"

"A. K. Shoemaker is an idiot! That man's poison is permeating our entire Center. It's a vile and deceitful pack of lies!" She was livid. She held herself in check for a moment, then returned to her golf bag and exchanged her five iron for a three wood.

"Mr. Garrott, you're lousing up my golf game. I've got to have a clear head to play this game, and Professor Shoemaker doesn't . . . we're not going to solve the old problem of here-dity-versus-environment out here anyway, so let's forget it."

"Certainly. That was a bit of a digression anyway. What kind of an ad campaign did you come up with to combat this problem?"

She swung and topped the ball, which skittered along the ground for about 100 yards. Then she took a deep breath, lined up another ball and stepped back. Henry had almost given up hope for a response when she said, "Very simple, actually. We used a direct approach. We went to the Beer Distillers Association and convinced a number of them to cooperate with our program.

"Have you noticed in the past two years, a number of TV beer ads showing happy, domestic scenes in black homes? The father comes home from work and the wife immediately puts him to work assembling the children's toy, then the wife slips him a beer. Or the one I especially liked showed a birthday party for the grandfather figure, with lots of his children and grandchildren around to help him celebrate; and, of course, all the adults were toasting each other with the beer the company was pushing."

"Yes, I do remember. That was your doing?"

"You bet. Bertha came up with the concept and I translated it into a playable domestic vignette. The whole appeal, obviously, was to make family togetherness attractive and desirable to the black viewer, from age sixteen to forty. Since beer ads are naturally tailored to appeal to our target age group, it was a logical marriage."

"Fantastic! Were you actually able to determine if your campaign was making any difference?"

"After one year's programming, we tested, and there was enough attitude change to interest the Ad Council. Two years would have been more significant, I'm sure."

"And what did the advertiser get out of all this?" Henry asked.

"Since the commercial served a dual purpose, the advertiser paid for one ad only, but was allowed a double tax deduction on that part of his advertising expense. Distillers advertise quite heavily, and it was a terrific incentive for them.

"We had marvelous campaigns lined up to deal with such problems as school violence, racial understanding, job skills, proper diet. All good ol' American goals."

"And Robinson and someone else put you out of business?"

"That's right," she said, and slammed the ball.

"I don't understand why Dr. Robinson would object to your program."

"We didn't either. It completely baffled us. Especially since he supported us in the beginning. Something or someone got to him to change his mind."

"Did he give you a specific reason?"

"Oh, yes. He said it was the old story of whites manipulating blacks, of the elite controlling the lives and destiny of the poor. I think he also brought up Aldous Huxley and *1984*, if memory serves me correctly."

"I see his point. Such a campaign could get out of hand, especially since it was secretive in nature."

She shook her head, "We had plenty of safeguards built in. We chose only goals everyone could accept. There was nothing political about it—but why am I standing here defending it? It's over and done with."

"What was it, about three years down the drain?"

"At least. We thought we'd just let Robinson rant and rave. We had our ducks in line. But we weren't planning on Begelman being ill or A. K. Shoemaker turning on us."

"You're sure it was Shoemaker who voted against the project?"

"Of course. Who else would it be?"

"He told me he supported it."

"And you believed him?" She smiled and shook her head slowly, as though she were questioning Henry's intelligence.

"There is one other aspect that may have played a part in the vote." Henry paused to see if her curiosity was simmering.

"What might that be?" she asked, fiddling with her glove.

"The fight for the emphasis and direction of the entire Center. General Kilbourne established the Center primarily as a research center in the social sciences, but it appears the biological scientists are taking over. If there was going to be a struggle between the two groups, it would probably show itself over funding."

Dr. Jones looked thoughtfully out of the corner of her eye, then shook her head slowly. "No, I've never gotten the feeling of any friction. Begelman was most helpful, and the young Professor Ballard was very enthusiastic. He wanted to know every detail of our Cleveland operation. He also made several helpful suggestions. No, if anything, I'd say there were very good feelings for the most part. There's never been a question of funding. We've always had our separate sources."

"So this was the first time you were attempting to draw funds from a common pool."

"Yes, I guess it was," she said thoughtfully.

"One more question, if I may: Why were you headquartering your operations out of Cleveland? I thought the advertising industry was primarily centered in New York and the West Coast."

"Three reasons. I used to be in advertising in that city, so I knew my way around. Also, we were close to a lot of the industries we needed in order to get into sample mailings."

"You mean soaps, toothpaste?"

"Everything," she chuckled. "We really had plans . . . ."

She struck another ball. She had her swing grooved now,

and the ball had a low, straight trajectory until it got about half way to the target. At that point, it started climbing, then floating. The ball seemed to hang in space for a moment, then drop helplessly to the ground in front of the 210-yard marker, next to all its little white friends. It was the kind of shot high handicappers, like Henry, only dream about.

"We were planning," she continued, "to solicit responses from identified problem teenagers on the effectiveness of samples we would mail to them. That was part of our psychological testing program we were into for progress analysis."

"Sounds very ambitious and complicated."

"Yes, it would have been fun. I wonder if Robinson really knows what he has done . . . bless his little heart."

Henry gave her a surprised look. "Dr. Jones, you haven't heard what's happened? Dr. Robinson is dead."

"Dead? You're kidding!"

Her reaction seemed genuine enough. She smiled, gave a little laugh, then twisted her head slightly to indicate disbelief. Henry proceeded to tell her about the events of Saturday, including the arrest of Shoemaker. She took it all in quietly.

"I'm sorry I didn't tell you before. I just assumed you knew," Henry explained.

"Well, well. What do you think of that. Things do change, don't they?" She methodically lined up three more balls.

Henry couldn't help but think that the change that had come about would only help the social scientists; the two people who were now out of the way were the two whom Dr. Jones said voted against her pet project.

She hit another ball. This one hooked slightly, and it rolled off to the left of her pattern area.

"Dr. Jones, what did Bertha Corbut die from?"

She looked up quickly and seemed to sense the worst implications of Henry's question. "Mr. Garrott, what possible connection could that have to your investigation of our funding?"

"None, directly, that I know of, but—"

"Why did Mr. McCarthy bring you here anyway? What can you do for us that he can't do himself?"

"I'm here to help him with the financial system—primarily, the General Fund."

"Then, I suggest you stick to that topic." She glanced at

her watch. "You'll have to excuse me now. I'm happy to cooperate with the administration of the Center, but under the circumstances, I must insist that any future questions you may
have will be answered in Mr. McCarthy's office—with my lawyer present. Good-bye, Mr. Garrott."

"Yes, fine. Thank you," Henry replied demurely. He rose
and returned the chair to its original spot.

As he walked away, he looked over his shoulder in time to
watch Dr. Jones hook a ball badly up into the nearby hillside.
Rather than follow the flight of the ball, she stood quietly with
her head down, gently tapping the ground with her three
wood. Henry wondered what kind of golf round she had ahead
of her, and if she would ever think kindly of him.

There was a map of the area in the glove compartment of
his rental car, so Henry located the Center, and the street
where McCarthy must have been running Saturday morning.
Tracing along a back road to the Center, he found a spot
where the two roads came within a quarter mile of each other.
He was going to the Center anyway, so he decided to try the
back road and survey the terrain.

He soon realized why the two roads appeared to serpentine
on the map, and why there were no connecting roads. Both
roads were built along hillsides and were separated by a common ravine. The hillsides were steep, and covered with scrub
oak and heavy underbrush. There were no signs of trails, or access routes, from one hillside to the other, as far as Henry
could observe. Judging from this, and McCarthy's question-
able physical condition, Henry all but eliminated McCarthy's
direct involvement in Dr. Robinson's death.

As he drew near the Center, Henry noticed the sound of a
siren. He spotted a large fire truck slowly making its way up
the main road. Henry looked for a sign of smoke from the
Center, but could see none, then stepped on the gas.

He arrived to find the truck parked outside the office wing
of the building. Hoses were being connected and run into the
entrance. Professor Ballard was sitting on the low wall near the
entrance, resting his head on his arms, while Miss Matthews,
dressed in her Sunday best, stood next to him, trying to comfort him.

Ballard was sooty and dirty, and had burn marks on both

of his upturned hands. He was surrounded by boxes and desk drawers, filled mostly with paper, which he must have taken from somewhere in the building. Most of the material seemed unburned, but two large file drawers, full of scorched papers, were still smoldering.

When Ballard saw Henry approaching, he stood up. "Garrott, Mr. Garrott, why would anyone do such a thing? My papers, all my records . . . it doesn't make any sense."

"Did you get everything out?" Henry asked.

"No. My big file cabinet . . . it's still burning!"

"Is it locked?"

"Yes."

"Give me the key."

"I . . . I . . . don't know . . . my whole life's work." He looked off toward his office in a daze. Henry grabbed him by his shoulders.

"Listen, Ballard, maybe we can still save them. Where is the key?"

Ballard's eyes finally fixed on Henry, with some sign of recognition. "The key . . . I don't have it. I keep it hidden in my desk—but it's not there."

Henry raced into the Center, following the hose and the smoke down the corridor into Ballard's office. It was a large room adjoining a laboratory. Smoke poured from the top drawer of a large file set into the wall. Two firemen stood by with a large hose, as a third worked on the cabinet drawer with a crowbar.

"Wait, wait!" Henry called. "There are valuable papers in there. We've got to do everything we can to preserve them."

"Listen, buddy," the fireman with the crowbar called, "if we don't get this out, this whole inner wall's going to go." He took another whack at the drawer.

Henry grabbed him by the arm. "Listen, can't we try your CO_2 canister? We'll get a key over here as fast as we can."

Henry finally persuaded them to try the fire-retarding gas, especially since they were not making much headway on the drawers. They put the nozzle of their extinguisher into the corners and small holes of the drawers and by using short bursts of the gas so the already-damaged papers wouldn't blow around more than necessary, the smoke soon subsided.

Henry started toward the entrance where he had left Ballard and Miss Matthews, in hopes Miss Matthews would be able to locate a master key. She had anticipated this and he met her running toward him with the key in hand. After much jiggling and forcing, the hot drawers were all removed and placed in the center of the room. The papers in the top drawers were singed on the edges but were so tightly packed there appeared to be little damage to the important areas of the paper. The bottom drawer was a mass of ashes and fine soot. The other looked as if the material had turned to charcoal. As long as the papers were intact, Henry knew there were methods of saving the information.

He watched as the firemen started to spray the inner wall where the file drawers had been set. He asked and was assured by the leader that if the drawers flared up again, the flames would be smothered, and not doused with water, to prevent further damage to their contents. The heavy smoke forced Miss Matthews outside again. Henry followed.

A fireman was applying first aid to Ballard's hands; Henry came over and sat next to him. "I think we saved everything except the papers in the bottom drawer. What did you have in the bottom drawer?"

"What . . . let me see . . ."

Ballard blinked his eyes as if he were having trouble concentrating. "I'm not used to this sort of thing. Who would do a thing like this? Why?"

"I'd best call Mr. McCarthy," Miss Matthews said, wiping her eyes.

"Are you all right?" Henry asked.

"Yes, I'm fine," she assured him. "I'll go in the other entrance," she said, and disappeared around the corner of the building.

Ballard grimaced in pain as the last knot was tied on the bandages. The fireman said it looked like first- and second-degree burns only, but advised that a doctor examine the burns to guard against infection.

Henry asked Ballard if he had stored combustible chemicals in any of the drawers.

"No. Nothing like that. It had to be set by someone. There was nothing there but papers."

"Did you discover the fire?"

"Yes."

"How'd you happen to find it?" Henry asked.

"It was obvious," he blurted. "The flames were shooting right out of the cabinets; the big one in the wall and the little one by my desk."

"I mean, how did you happen to be at the Center on Sunday morning? Do you usually work on Sunday?"

"No, I don't. I heard on the car radio about Robinson's death and I got to wondering . . . ." His voice trailed off as he squirmed in his seat. He was obviously very uncomfortable.

"Do you want to lie down?"

"No, no. I'd rather sit up. I carried out these two." He gestured weakly at the file drawers nearby. "Funny, I didn't even feel the pain till I got 'em out here. Funny."

He stood up as if to walk about, but found himself a bit shaky, and sat right back down again. "I wish I were a child again so I could cry." He laughed. "I think it would help.

"Robinson sometimes had experiments going over the weekend, and I thought I'd better come back and check. My wife and I were on our way up to the high desert to see the wild flowers when we got the news."

"So you came back to check on an experiment he may have started?" Henry asked.

"Well, that and to be with Wilma, Robinson's wife. She doesn't know any people out here, and the four of us had been quite close. Say, wait!" Ballard seemed to snap into consciousness. "Greg Robinson used to keep materials in my big file. He was cramped for space, so I made room for him in my lower drawer. I kept the key in my desk so he could get at it whenever he needed. You don't suppose somebody was after his records, and not mine?"

"Possibly," Henry mused. "You don't suppose he stored any volatile materials in there?"

"Highly unlikely. We have special cabinets in the lab, right next door, for anything like that, and Robinson was very careful—very professional."

"And you say you couldn't find your key to the file?"

"No. I keep it on a hook in the knee hole of my desk, but it wasn't there. Of course I was in a bit of a hurry. I didn't spend a lot of time looking. I just grabbed these two drawers that are never locked and whatever else—"

"Was the location of that key common knowledge?"

"No, I don't think so. Robinson, my new lab assistant, and myself, I think, were the only ones—I don't know. McCarthy and Miss Matthews have the only master keys to every lock. I suppose anyone else working in the lab could have looked through the office windows and watched us get the key. But who would want to?"

"Apparently someone did. It appears to me the fire was started on the inside of the file. Unless there's an electrical short, or something else we don't know about now, it looks as if you are right—arson."

Henry looked over the two files on the wall next to Ballard. They seemed to contain mostly bundles of computer print-outs that had been scorched black by the slow burning. By moving his head around to get the sun's angle on the paper he could distinguish the shiny ink images of what appeared to be computer-typed addresses.

"Believe it or not, most of this is salvageable," Henry said. "I've had a little experience in salvaging documents, but it may not be necessary. Wouldn't most of this information be in your computer data bank?"

"A lot of it would . . . in one form or another."

Miss Matthews came down the steps still covering her nose and mouth. "I reached him. He didn't sound too happy, but he's on his way over. I also took the liberty of calling Mrs. Ballard. I hope you don't mind."

Ballard's eyes said otherwise, but he replied, "No, it's all right."

"She's trying to reach your doctor. Said she'll pick you up as soon as she can."

"Miss Matthews," Ballard called in a surprised voice. "It just dawned on me. What are *you* doing here? Aren't you usually in church at this hour?"

"Mr. Garrott needed some papers. I just dropped by for a moment."

"Well, I'm glad you did. Thank you for your help."

"You're welcome," she answered with an appreciative smile.

"Miss Matthews, there may be a problem with the computer data bank," Henry broke in. "I wonder, if it's not too much trouble, might I take a look at where you store your software?"

"Certainly."

The two of them started toward the building, but Ballard called, "Wait a minute." He rose to his feet and started following.

"Are you sure you're up to this?" Henry wondered.

"Yes. I'm more anxious than you are to find out. You couldn't tell if any of my discs were missing anyway. I should have fourteen."

They made their way into the computer room, and Miss Matthews opened the storage bin where the program discs were kept. There was a label on the edge of each disc pack, with the last name of the programmer and the number of the program. Ballard's discs were all in their alphabetical slots, and marked neatly, one through fourteen. There was a space for Robinson, but no discs.

"No discs," Henry mumbled, running his hand over the shelf.

Ballard thought for a moment. "That doesn't mean too much. He wasn't into computers. The only time I ever saw him in here was when he was running one of my programs, or Dr. Begelman's, for instructional purposes."

Ballard, a bit wobbly, started toward the exit. "Think I'll go out where there's a little more air."

"I think, just to be on the safe side, this should be kept under lock," Henry suggested, closing the lid. "And at least for the time being, Miss Matthews, you should keep the only key."

"I'll speak to Mr. McCarthy about that," she said.

"Fine."

The two of them caught up with Ballard and helped him back outside to their original spot on the low wall. They sat quietly and watched the firemen secure their equipment.

Henry was trying to sort out, in his own mind, the significance of this latest event. On the surface, it appeared someone killed Robinson because of what he knew, and now this person had taken the added precaution of destroying records which might also expose . . . that . . . something . . . . But perhaps there were two or more people involved. There had been a good deal of surreptitious thought and planning in all this—maybe too much for one person.

One of the firemen walked over with a notebook in hand to Jeffry Ballard. Henry moved over to Miss Matthew's side and started asking about Dr. Robinson's office. She had been a brick through all this, and Henry's admiration for her professionalism continued to grow.

Miss Matthews led Henry back into the office area to show him where Dr. Robinson's office was. The smoke had dissipated by then, and the firemen were mopping up. Robinson's office was right next to Ballard's, and opened into the lab in the same manner. All the offices were glass panelled so the professors could be at their desks and still keep an eye on activities in the lab. Conversely, anyone in the lab could easily see what was going on in the offices.

Henry tried the door to Dr. Robinson's and found it wasn't locked. It was a small room, and without a file cabinet. A few papers were strewn about the desk, but nothing to give the impression the place had been ransacked. Personal effects were in the center drawer, a few records and ledger books in the side drawers. Henry noticed a man's jacket hanging on a hook in the corner of the room. In the right-hand breast pocket was Dr. Robinson's wallet with thirteen dollars still in it. The picture section featured the smiling likeness of a striking black woman, no doubt his wife. Another snapshot showed Dr. Robinson and his wife at a picnic somewhere, with Jeffry and Tena Ballard. So much for Shoemaker's theory of Ballard's "deep-seated hatred of blacks."

Shoemaker! He'd forgotten about him. This fire had to remove suspicion from him now.

On the floor below the coat rack was a small doctor's bag. Henry put it on the desk so Miss Matthews could see everything he was doing. Inside, along with the usual medical paraphernalia, were three small bottles Henry presumed to be the antibiotics Robinson had brought along to administer to him Saturday morning.

"Does anything look unusual or out of place about this room, Miss Matthews?"

"I've rarely been in here, so I really can't say."

"Sit down for a moment Miss Matthews, would you?"

They both sat.

"It was mentioned the other day that you had said Dr. Robinson had been upset about something. Can you tell me what that might be?"

"Mr. Garrott . . . you are placing me in a very awkward position. I really don't understand your status here."

"Didn't Vern McCarthy talk to you about me?"

"Yes, but he really didn't make too much sense."

"I see. Well, there are monies missing from the General Fund—a substantial amount, and Vern brought me on board to find out quietly what is going on. We were acquaintances when we were both in government service. Now I have reason to believe all these events may be linked together."

"I see," she said, her face tense.

"You were with Gen. Kilbourne when he founded the Center, weren't you?"

"Long before that. I was with him during the war years when he headed the National Propaganda Program for the Defense Department. I was a W.A.C."

"Is that so?" Henry tried to sound as enthusiastic as he could, hoping to draw her out.

"Yes, those were exciting days."

"You were his personal secretary then?"

"A group of us girls went with him into private industry. We were pretty much interchangeable. Three of us made the move out here. I'm the last. He used to call us his 'Chief Administrators.' I'm the last of the 'Chief Administrators.' " She smiled. "He was a marvelous man."

"He must have been."

"He could do things—accomplish things—just from the sheer power of his personality. He was so good, such a great heart. People could sense that."

"What do you think of the operation of the Center now?"

"Mr. MacKenzie was able to hold things together for a few years, but after the General died . . . well, it just wasn't the same."

"You mean, you object to the currect direction?" Henry queried.

"I mean, the *lack* of direction—the void that has been left. Oh, I don't mean to disparage the efforts of your Mr. McCarthy and the others. I'm sure they mean well, but they've lost the 'big picture,' if you will. Why, the General used to call a group of us into his office in the evening after work—Mr. McCarthy's office—and he would look out at the ocean and just chat and ramble on about his dreams for the country, and the world. We would leave just tingling with excitement. It was sheer joy to come to work each day. There was hope. . . .

"Now we have so many things going on. Little people mixing things in test tubes no one else knows anything about, and people groveling after the almighty dollar. Now, the bad feelings this Shoemaker theory is spreading about, both in and out of the Center—it's like a poison. Such things would just never have happened with the General around. People nowadays don't have the big heroes we used to have—they criticize, and pick, and find fault until everyone is on the same level, but we're missing out. We're missing out on a lot. The big man could accomplish so much we just can't do anymore."

They sat in silence for a moment. Henry watched her hands while she folded and unfolded her Sunday gloves, seemingly lost in her past. For the first time that day, he remembered how old she was. She looked so neat and crisp, and conducted herself so efficiently, that it was easy to forget she was nearing retirement age—until one looked at the telltale hands. Henry guessed she had given her life to her work, and to her own unique form of hero worship. Now, in her declining years, she had to watch most of her dreams and illusions crumble. He wished he could somehow restore her dreams.

"But you were asking me about Dr. Robinson," she said, slipping her gloves into her small purse. "I really can't tell you much. Approximately two weeks ago, I found him at my desk—I'd just stepped out for a moment—and he was going over the travel records. We have an account with a local travel agency, and I make all the travel arrangements for the Center's staff people. There's nothing secret about the records. It just startled me to find him there. I asked if I could help him. He said he was concerned about what was going on in Cleveland."

"Cleveland?" Henry asked. "Do you remember his exact words?"

She thought a moment. "I think he said, 'I'm worried about what's happening in Cleveland.' "

"Was there anything in your record book that interested him?"

"I don't think so. The only connections I had made to Cleveland were for Dr. Jones and Bertha Corbut, and that had been months ago."

"Had Dr. Jones traveled to Cleveland since their project had fallen through?"

"No, I'm sure not; well, as sure as I can be. There's nothing to prevent anyone from purchasing his own ticket."

"Cleveland. Did he say anything else? Anything to give a clue about why he was worried?"

She searched her memory again. "No. I remember how disorganized and preoccupied he seemed, and what a change that was from the way he acted when he first came here.

"I think some of the staff voted to accept him here just to spite Shoemaker, and then were pleasantly surprised at how nicely he fit in."

"Shoemaker gave me the impression he didn't think Robinson was qualified to do research work."

"Oh, Shoemaker!" She dismissed him with a flip of her hand.

"I'd like to know more about the project he was working on. How would you suggest I go about that?"

"We might look over his log book. Didn't I see that in this top right-hand drawer here?"

Henry pulled it out and scanned through it.

"Also, I'm sure you'd want to talk with the lab assistant. A young girl . . . Charlie something. She worked for both Professor Ballard and Dr. Robinson. Dr. Begelman worked very closely with Dr. Robinson in the early months, but after his stroke, he asked to be relieved of his other duties to concentrate on a book, so I question how much real help he could be."

"All right; thank you," Henry said, still studying the log. The early entries were very complete and detailed, showing graphs and time charts of the activities Henry surmised were cultures with different forms of sickle-cell anemia strains. In late April, the entries became sporadic, and by May they stopped completely. There was a marked difference in the handwriting of the late entries. They became large abbreviated notes, nearly illegible, while the early entries were all carefully constructed sentences in a small, clear hand. Something must have been preoccupying his mind, Henry thought; something of such a serious nature that important experiments were going unfinished or unrecorded.

"While you are going over this," Miss Matthews said, rising, "why don't I find you those profiles you had requested?"

"Oh, yes. Thank you," Henry replied, and handed her a list of the six people on whom he wanted information. "Could I ask you to do the same on General Kilbourne? I'd really like to know more about the man."

This obviously pleased Miss Matthews, and she hurried on her way.

Most of the data Henry found in the drawers was of such a technical nature he couldn't understand it. There was one published paper, however, which had possibilities. It compared the work Dr. Begelman had done toward defining and controlling Tay-Sachs, a uniquely Jewish disease, with the work Dr. Robinson was doing with sickle-cell anemia, an almost exclusively negro disease. He made note of the publication and date in case he needed it later.

Loud voices from Ballard's office next door grabbed Henry's attention, and he rushed over, expecting to see the place in flames again. It was Vern McCarthy, carrying on a heated conversation with the firemen. He sounded as if he was accusing them of creating the initial disturbance.

After Miss Matthews' description of her Gen. Kilbourne, Henry couldn't help but compare the two men. Vern McCarthy came in a poor second.

After the clamor subsided, and McCarthy was identified as

the Director in residence, the fireman, who introduced himself as Inspector Murdock, led Henry and McCarthy to the holes in the wall where the files had been. He flicked on his flashlight and pointed at the unfinished cement floor behind the wall.

"You see that?" Murdock said.

"I'm afraid I don't know what it is we're supposed to be seeing," Henry confessed.

"That—that wax and the curlicue thing on the back wall there."

He pointed again and they recognized what appeared to be a small puddle of wax and a burnt string or wire.

"What is that supposed to be?" McCarthy asked.

"We can't be sure yet, but it looks like parafin, and the twisted black wire is probably a fast-burning fuse."

"You mean a poor man's arson kit?" Henry asked.

"That's right. We'll test that wax and if it's the type used to make a candle, we've got an arson case on our hands. I'm almost certain that black wire used to be a fuse. The candle burns down and starts the fuse. The fuse, which is very hot, ignites some crumpled paper, and whoosh!"

"So the fire could have been set last night, then," Henry suggested.

"Sure. Or even earlier."

"Could a candle burn as long as twenty-four hours before it set off the fuse?"

"Oh, yes, with a slow-burning candle and very little draft, it's possible."

"Is there any way to determine when it was started?"

"Nnnooo, I don't think there is. We can check the wax and estimate the candle length, but most of a candle is fuel that actually burns up, so there's really no accurate way. If we hadn't stopped this fire when we did, that wax would have burned too."

"Why do you want to know that?" McCarthy asked Henry.

"Because of Shoemaker. The only logical time he could have started the fire would have been before Dr. Robinson fell. I doubt if he would have had time later."

"There's no doubt that he did then," McCarthy said.

"Sounds to me like you people better be talking to the police," Murdock said, and headed back toward his crew. "Don't touch that area; we'll be taking pictures," he called.

"What's this going to do to our insurance?" McCarthy yelled back, but the only answer he got was a sarcastic laugh.

Henry mused over this new possibility.

"Well, what do you think?" McCarthy demanded.

"The more I think about this, the less I think Shoemaker was involved."

"Of course he was; the police don't go around arresting people on a lark, you know."

"Then what was it that Shoemaker was trying to hide? Why would he start this fire?"

"Maybe the two events aren't related," McCarthy shrugged.

"Oh, come now . . . and why burn anything? Whoever started this fire had a key to the files. Why not just remove the incriminating evidence and be done with it? Why start a fire that would attract a lot of attention?"

McCarthy scratched his already rumpled hair. "Maybe this was just a smoke screen—a diversionary tactic to get us confused."

"Yes, or maybe whoever did it didn't know what he was supposed to be looking for so he decided to burn everything. Such a description hardly fits a scientist like Shoemaker, though, does it?"

"Listen, leave that end of it alone," McCarthy said. "Just do what I've asked you to do and leave that problem to the police."

"All right, but in the meantime, keep the computer programs under lock and key. They might be next. And I think all of Ballard's programs should be gone over for content. Do you have someone familiar with his work who could do that?"

"Yes, I'll take care of it, but in the meantime, remember . . . low profile."

"I understand."

"What are your plans now?"

"I'm still questioning people who were on the signature card."

"Okay, who've you seen so far?"

"Just Dr. Jones, since I talked to you. Say, what did Bertha Corbut die from?"

"A bad combination of alcohol and prescription medicine. She was on something to calm her nerves, and, supposedly, when she and Jones heard the bad news about their funding request, they had a little drinking bout to soothe their ruffled feathers. Bertha Corbut never woke up the next morning. Why?"

"When I asked Dr. Jones about it, she just clammed up."

McCarthy shook his head. "Man, you still don't get it, do you? Leave this murder business to the police. Just find out about the missing money. That's all; that's all!"

"But the one thing seems to be tied in with the other."

"All right—so what if it is? Just draw the line and concern yourself only with the money."

"Why?"

"Why? Because that's what I'm asking you to do." McCarthy was almost stomping his feet, he was so irritated.

"I'm concerned with getting at the truth, aren't you?"

McCarthy closed his eyes and took a deep breath. "I'm concerned with holding this place together, and at this point I really don't care how I do it. Oh, I don't mean that. All I'm asking—expecting—is for you to show a little loyalty. You gotta look at the big picture."

"You can save that State Department jargon, because I don't look at the big picture anymore. I only look at the big, big picture."

McCarthy growled, "My, my, it must be tough to be so holy."

Henry smiled. "The yoke is easy, Vern. The yoke is easy."

Leaving McCarthy to fuss about the fire sprinkler system that didn't work, Henry wandered into the Great Hall while waiting for Miss Matthews. All the debris had been cleaned up and yellow chalk outlined the spot where Dr. Robinson had fallen. The double helix model was in better shape than Henry remembered. Except for the missing section directly below the scaffold, it had weathered the affair quite well. Outside, the fire truck's engine revved up and moved away; the sound reverberating through the Big Hall made goose bumps stand out on Henry's forearms. The place was just too large for comfort.

Miss Matthews came out of her office and presented Henry with a large manila envelope. "This should keep you busy for some time," she said. They walked together outside in time to see Tena Ballard helping her husband into the car. As they watched the Ballards drive away Henry commented, "I take it he was already carrying things out when you arrived this morning."

"Yes. I made him stop when I saw his hands," she said.

"Then he must have put in the alarm."

"Yes, I suppose he did."

"We're fortunate to have such a prompt and efficient fire department," Henry murmured half-heartedly. Something was troubling him about the whole affair, as though he were watching a scene in a play he didn't understand. Once, in Stockholm, he made the mistake of attending a contemporary play in Swedish, a language he knew nothing about. Not only did each event in the play seem meaningless, but there seemed to be no relationship between events. Most frustrating of all, the people around him were enjoying themselves immensely.

Was there someone now enjoying himself immensely? No. That was part of the problem. These weren't malicious people. They were not the kind that steal money, or murder with brute violence, or start fires that could end up costing millions. Either someone was acting way out of his normal personality pattern, or an outside element could be involved—a split personality. Yes, a highly intelligent, dedicated person working under stress, pushed to the point that a second, counter-personality emerges who is completely counter-productive to the first personality.

Perhaps someone like Ballard . . . certainly there was the stress. The second personality takes over and kills a friend of the first personality. Later it burns the very records the first personality spent years developing. The first personality senses there is something wrong at the Center; consciously he doesn't even know the other personality exists, but instinctively he senses something wrong. He rushes to the Center and desperately tries to save his life's work from destruction, without even realizing his unique relationship to the destroyer.

The destroyer could also have embezzled the money, intending to start a life of his own. That also could explain Dr. Robinson's dying words. He found out about the two personalities and cried out, "Don't let *them* kill us." It made sense . . . it was logical . . .

These thoughts raced through Henry's head while he was carrying on light conversation with Miss Matthews and driving away from the Center. Miss Matthews had invited him to attend church services with her and he accepted. He followed her car down the hill into the church parking lot, parked his car and found himself sitting in a back row pew, hardly realizing he was doing it. This new theory fascinated him; he couldn't take his mind off it.

The choir sang a Vivaldi anthem which finally grabbed Henry's attention. It was a joyous cascade of praise and adulation for the one great and eternal God. It exhilarated Henry. Before his conversion, he had difficulty understanding the value or need of all the singing in church gatherings, but now he knew why. Believers sing because they can't help it. It's such a natural thing to do, once one sees the beauty and grace of it all.

The music woke Henry up, but the sermon soon chased him back to his mental wanderings. The minister, a middle-aged Scotsman, seemed quite taken with his own diction. He revelled in the use of words like "justification" and "propitiation," leaving spiritual babes like Henry out in the cold. When the speaker hit "amelioration," Henry was gone.

Ballard's destructive personality could easily have lured Dr. Robinson to the Center, assuming the destructive personality knew about "Mr. Nice Guy," but "Mr. Nice Guy" didn't know about "Mr. Destruction." Henry wondered if such split personalities really operated that way. It did seem logical that Mr. Nice Guy would say to himself, "I must not hate blacks. It's immoral and irrational." Mr. Nice Guy would suppress the feeling gnawing away at him until it manifested itself in a second personality whose dominant trait was destruction and revenge. Sounded good. But what was wrong with it?

The main objection had to be probability. Such personality splits rarely occur. "One in a million" seemed to stick in Henry's mind. Even then, would a second personality be so totally destructive? He recalled that each of the split personalities he had read about had some redeeming traits. Such a Jekyll-and-Hyde split seemed incongruous. And how did Mr. Destruction put the ripped lab coat into the bottom drawer of Shoemaker's locked office? Such a theory hardly explained Dr. Robinson's strange behavior of dropping his lab experiments in the last month. He would probably agonize over committing a friend for psychiatric treatment, but since he was a doctor, he certainly would have done it rather than wait.

Then too, there was the Cleveland business. Ballard had been to Cleveland, but what other possible tie-in could there be? After all, Dr. Robinson did say, "I'm worried about what's going on in Cleveland," while according to Miss Matthews, Ballard had not been away from the Center in the last five months.

Things to do: find out if Jeffry Ballard had any blackout periods recently, and find out where he was early Saturday morning.

Judging from the coughing and the head-nodding around him, Henry realized he was not the only one in the congregation whose mind was wandering. He longed for the direct language of the book of Acts and wondered how the dynamics of Christianity ever got institutionalized.

After the service, Henry bid Miss Matthews good-bye and left quickly. He wanted to swing by the County Hospital in hopes of finding the Ballards still in the Emergency Room. The chances were good that Jeffry Ballard's doctor would not be on duty on Sunday morning. Seeing what appeared to be the Ballards' car in the Emergency lot, Henry went in and looked about.

"Well, hello, how's that left wrist coming along?" the young doctor who had treated Henry asked, as he came hurrying by down the corridor.

"Just fine."

"Probably stiff now, right?"

"Not too bad."

"We got another chap in here from the Center this morning. What are you people doing up there, playing war games?"

Henry chuckled. "Looks that way, doesn't it? Could you show me where he is?"

The doctor waved toward a treatment room and hurried on his way.

Henry knocked gently on the door; Tena Ballard opened it almost immediately. Jeffry Ballard sat on the examining table in the small room, his shirt draped over his shoulders. The new bulkier bandages on his hands indicated he had already been treated.

"Hello, there. Getting along all right?" Henry questioned softly.

"Oh, yes, thank you," Tena assured.

Henry slipped into the room and stood quietly, not knowing exactly how to begin.

"Nice of you to come by," Tena said. "The doctor says his burns are not too serious. If he can keep his hands immobilized a day or two, he shouldn't have any problems. We're just waiting for some medication."

"Feeling better?" Henry asked Ballard directly.

He smiled. "Yes, thank you."

"Burns can really take the starch out of you. I was wondering if you were up to a couple more questions."

"Certainly."

"Saturday morning, about the time Dr. Robinson fell, you weren't anywhere around the Center, were you? Such as in your office?"

"No." Ballard laughed. "That was quite early, wasn't it?"

"Yes, around six-thirty, seven o'clock."

"No, no, we like to sleep in on Saturdays."

"But don't you remember, dear," Tena broke in, "Friday night we set the alarm so you could get up and watch that TV program."

"Oh, yes, I forgot about that."

"What program was this, at 7:00?"

"Six-thirty. It was an instructional TV class. They were showing a film called 'The Discovery of the Double Helix.' "

"And you watched it?" Henry asked.

"Yes."

"I really have to hand it to you. I think if I watched anything as dry as a science program at that hour of the morning on Saturday, I'd fall asleep." Henry fumbled with his car keys and looked for a graceful way to say it. "You didn't fall asleep, did you?"

"No, I didn't. Once I'm up, I'm up. Besides I was quite upset. They made several critical errors in their historical development of the search for the double helix. Our Dr. Begelman was hardly mentioned. Why, if it hadn't been for him, and his early work with the electron microscope, we'd still be searching."

"I take it you didn't think much of the program."

"It was very well done, but the writers had simply not done their homework. I immediately shot off a letter to the station, and to the producer listed on the closing credits, informing them of their errors. Not that it will do any good."

"Why do you want to know if he was in his office?" Tena asked. "Was someone seen in there?"

"Someone was in there who shouldn't have been. We're not exactly sure when. But you're certain you weren't there at all Saturday, either early morning or later?"

"No, I wasn't. About the only time I go in on the weekend is if I have an experiment in progress, and I have nothing going right now."

"I see." Henry stepped toward the door, then turned back to face the Ballards. "This next question may seem a bit unusual, so let me give you the background. Dr. Robinson had been acting in a strange or unusual manner in the last month or so, and we were wondering if there was a physical problem—you know, fumes from a lab experiment or something which might have affected his balance or judgment. Since you and Dr. Robinson worked closely together, in the same part of the lab and all, I was wondering if you'd noticed any change in your own health."

Ballard thought a moment. "No, I don't think so."

"Think carefully," Henry urged. "No dizziness or blackouts? No periods that you can't remember!"

"Certainly not."

"Mrs. Ballard, have you noticed any change in him?"

She thought seriously for a moment. "Yes, I have noticed a change, come to think of it. He gets better looking every time I see him!"

Ballard answered, in a heavy hillbilly drawl, "Ah shucks, maw, you're makin' me blush."

They all laughed at the little joke, and the Ballards kissed lightly.

"Seriously," Ballard spoke, "I doubt if anything in the lab could cause such an effect. We seldom have an occasion to use toxic chemicals."

"How about Dr. Robinson?"

"Well, of course, I can't speak for him, but I seriously doubt it."

"You don't know for sure? I thought you two worked closely—"

"We certainly used to. I spent a good deal of time getting him started when he first came here."

"And lately?" Henry asked.

"Lately, as you've indicated, he's been very distant—almost morose. He's asked me a few technical questions, but no socializing."

"Any idea why?"

"I think his research was progressing badly. He was working on a new detection system for sickle-cell anemia carriers, and I think the task was too much for him. He didn't have the money to do everything he wanted to do, and I think the enormity of the task just overwhelmed him."

"There were personal problems too," Tena Ballard put in.

"Now honey, we don't know that for a fact."

"What kind of personal problems?"

"I think they were getting a divorce."

"Divorce? You mean Dr. Robinson and his wife?"

"Tena," Ballard objected. "The man is dead. Let's not start any unfounded rumors."

"Well, it's true. I can't say for certain. But I'd bet anything it's true. Women can sense things like that. We used to be very close with the Robinsons. We were all rather lonely when they moved out here from back east, and well, we just hit it off to-

gether. But lately . . . well, they've been avoiding us. A husband and wife usually do avoid other couples they've both
been friendly with when break-ups occur.''

"I see," Henry acknowledged.

"And she's made some comments—just little snide re-
marks that made me think she wasn't pleased with Greg.''

"Tena, I'm surprised at you," Ballard said with a taut smile
that wasn't all friendly. "I've never seen this side of you before.''

"Dear, it's our obligation to tell what we know. After all,
most accidents occur when people are upset about personal
problems. I'm not being catty.''

"Have you been to see Mrs. Robinson yet?" inquired
Henry.

"No. Jeff wanted to go this morning but then this happened.''

Henry jiggled his keys again. He couldn't think of anything
more to ask, so he headed for the door. "Thanks for your help.
You've been most kind, under the circumstances.''

"You're welcome," Ballard said. "But I wouldn't take too
seriously what my wife just told you. It's really all specula-
tion.''

"Women can tell about things like that," Tena argued.
"Another person you should talk to about Greg Robinson is
Charlie Bell, his lab assistant.''

"Oh yes, I'd like to see her," Henry said.

Ballard glanced at his wife with disgust just for an instant,
but long enough to give Henry the impression Tena suspected
a romantic link between Dr. Robinson and the lab assistant.
Jeffry Ballard was putting down the idea.

"Do you know how I might reach her?"

"No," Ballard said. "She has an unlisted number, and her
street address isn't the same as the one she gave us at the
Center. I had to reach her one weekend so I drove out to the
address she had on her employment card; it was an empty lot.
She's very secretive.''

"The plot thickens, doesn't it, Mr. Garrott?" Tena Ballard
grinned.

Henry said good-bye again, went out, closed the door behind him and waited, expecting to hear a spat between the Ballards, but nothing materialized. They had been quite outgoing toward him—quite a change from the Friday night dinner party.

Was something troubling them Friday night, or . . . were they glib today in order to cover up something? Those two were intelligent enough to keep anyone guessing indefinitely if they chose. Why try to second guess them?

He decided the split personality theory was a washout, and that was what he came over to find out about.

Henry wanted to talk with the girl, Charlie. It would be a simple matter to get hold of her unlisted phone number. A call to the phone company using his old government emergency code—they wouldn't have changed that yet—and they would give the number to him. He rejected the idea as quickly as he had thought of it. If living with a strict conscience was his handicap, he decided he would live with it.

Wilma Robinson's condominium was in a cluster of new units, all done in a modern Spanish motif with lots of wrought iron gates, and fountains that didn't work. It too was on a hillside not far from the Center, and was arranged for a maximum ocean view. Henry was almost persuaded his was the only house in Southern California without a view of the ocean.

He cleared his throat as he approached the door. Except that he needed to be discreet, he had not planned what he was going to say. A tall black man in a dark grey silk suit answered the doorbell.

"Yes?"

"I wonder if I might speak with Mrs. Robinson."

"Are you the Postal Inspector?"

"What? No, I'm not," Henry said.

"What is it about? Mrs. Robinson has had a bad shock . . ."

"Yes, I know. I'm here about the death of her husband."

"Under the circumstances I don't think—" He started closing the door on Henry, but stopped when a woman's voice behind him said:

"It's all right, Jimmy. Let him in."

Henry entered the living room in time to see Mrs. Robinson rising from the couch. She was a tall, slender girl, reaching almost six feet in her low-heeled shoes. She was dressed in jeans and a loose-fitting, Russian peasant blouse. Her eyes were red and puffy and she wore a sullen expression; but she seemed cordial, and offered Henry a seat.

Henry proceeded with his usual introduction and responded to the usual questions about his activities. He was working for the Center, he explained, investigating a financial matter which might be related to her husband's death. The silk suit was introduced as Jimmy Dill, her Los Angeles attorney. He was at first a bit hostile, and seemed quite protective of Wilma Robinson.

"I was the one who called your husband early yesterday morning," Henry said, showing his bandaged hand. "I needed a doctor and he was the only one in town I knew. I hope I didn't disturb you, calling at that hour."

"I didn't know about it. There's no extension in my room."

"I see. Mrs. Robinson, your husband sounded like he was already up and ready to leave the house for the Center."

She shrugged, "Maybe so. I was sleeping."

"So you didn't know he was going to the Center?"

"No."

"He sounded as if he was meeting someone at the Center. Do you have any idea who it might have been?"

Jimmy Dill interrupted. "Dr. Robinson had not been confiding in his wife lately."

"I see," Henry said—but he didn't. He was frustrated by the presence of the attorney and the few short answers he was getting from the youthful widow. He had trouble estimating the age of blacks, but from her hands, and the few words she had spoken, Henry guessed she was in her early twenties, if that.

"Mrs. Robinson, we've been concerned about your husband's activities of the last several weeks. Several of his acquaintances at the Center have commented that his actions had been . . . well, different than in the past. Can you think of anything that might have precipitated this change?"

Wilma shot a glance at her lawyer, thought a moment, then shook her head.

"He never mentioned being concerned about something going on at the Center that wasn't quite right?"

"He never talked much about his work," she said.

Henry had started formulating another question when Wilma sighed. Her lower lip started quivering and she excused herself to get a Kleenex.

When she returned Henry said, "I'm sorry to trouble you at a time like this, but anything you can tell us might be of help."

"It's all right," she said and waved him on.

"Had you noticed any change in your husband? Anything unusual?"

Again she looked to Jimmy Dill, then said, "Well, lately I've been thinking he was gonna start passin'."

"Passing—you mean passing bad checks?" Henry asked.

She looked at Jimmy Dill with a smile, then gave a tired laugh and flopped back against the couch backrest.

" 'Passing,' Mr. Garrott, is a term we blacks use for passing ourselves off as whites," Jimmy Dill explained.

"Oh, of course."

"Dr. Robinson apparently had been using some kind of cream on his skin to bleach it, and Mrs. Robinson felt if they were to move back east, Dr. Robinson was about to pass himself off for white."

"To bleach his skin? I didn't know that was possible."

"He was doing something, because he was definitely turning lighter," Dill insisted.

Wilma nodded in agreement.

"And it would be simple to get the hair straightened."

Henry tried to recall Dr. Robinson's image to his mind. He was rather light-skinned, as he remembered, but with a hefty head of kinky hair—the nose and mouth only slightly negroid.

"Why would he want to do that? I mean, here he was a successful professional man, apparently accepted as he was. What would be his purpose in wanting to be white?"

Again Wilma and Jimmy Dill exchanged glances reinforcing Henry's strong feeling they were withholding something.

"It still helps to be white in some circles, Mr. Garrott," Jimmy Dill said.

"Had he mentioned anything about moving back east?"

"Well, no," Wilma admitted. "Not in so many words."

"But you thought he might be . . ." Henry left it open to see if she would finish for him.

"I thought he might be leaving me," Wilma whimpered, and covered her face to cry. She sat silently for a moment, as though she were recovering, but then she gave a long involuntary inhaling sob and rushed from the room.

"I guess this was a mistake," Henry said. "I never should have come."

"Yes, it's a little early," Jimmy Dill agreed; "although she'll be leaving soon. The Robinson family wants the body flown back east for the burial."

"You're here to help with the arrangements?"

"It's turned out that way. Originally I was called in to file separation papers."

"On behalf of Dr. Robinson?" Henry asked.

"No. Mrs. Robinson."

The expression on Henry's face apparently called for further clarification, because Jimmy Dill smiled and continued, "I know what you're thinking. She's still . . ." He glanced toward the hallway to see if she was out of earshot. Then in a softer voice, "She was still very much in love with her husband. It happens a lot in my business. A wife starts divorce proceedings against the husband just to bring him to his senses. Sometimes it works; usually it doesn't."

Henry shook his head, then rubbed his neck. "This whole affair is getting complicated."

Jimmy Dill chuckled. "Life is like that." He rose with Henry and walked him to the door.

"At least they got that Shoemaker. If that's any consolation."

"I'm not so sure he's the one who was—"

"He's not?" Jimmy interrupted. "Is that why you was askin' about who he was meeting?"

"Partly."

The two men looked at each other in the doorway for a moment, then Jimmy reached for a letter on the coffee table.

"Then maybe you better take a look at this. I thought the whole thing was cut and dried. This was in the mailbox yesterday noon."

Henry looked at the short letter on official post office stationery, addressed to Dr. Gregory Robinson. The heart of the letter read:

Regarding your letter of May 23rd I have asked our Los Angeles office to look into the matter, since they are closer to your location.

An agent should be contacting you within a week for the purpose of questioning you, and the other parties involved. Tampering with the U.S. mails is a serious offense, Dr. Robinson, and you may rest assured, if your charges can be substantiated, appropriate action will follow.

It was signed by a postal administrator in the San Francisco office.

"I don't know if this has any bearing on his death, but it appears to me Dr. Robinson felt his or someone else's mail was being tampered with," Jimmy Dill said.

"Yesss . . .'the other parties' could mean it was mail at the Center."

"Does this help you any?" Dill asked.

"It's one more question in a very long series of questions. What I'd like to find is a few answers."

"We were given to understand the matter was cut and dried." Dill repeated himself absently, "Mr. McCarthy told Wilma it was this Shoemaker character. I never thought twice about the letter."

"The police don't know about it?"

"No. I don't think so anyway. Wilma said they just came by to verify what time the doctor left for the Center. They got the same answer you got.

"I think every black in the country would like to see Shoemaker guilty—at least everyone who knows about his theories. What makes you say he's not the one?"

"For one thing, there was an arson fire at the Center this morning, and many valuable papers were damaged, including a drawer full of Dr. Robinson's material. It would have been very difficult for Shoemaker to have started it."

"Unless, of course, he was conspiring with someone else."

"Yes, I hadn't thought of that," Henry mused.

Dill retrieved the letter from Henry and slowly returned it

to the envelope. "Sit down for a minute, will you?" he asked Henry, and moved toward the closed door in the hallway. He rapped softly and went into the other room when Wilma answered. Henry could hear their muffled voices for a good two minutes; spent the time surveying the living room appointments.

The Robinsons apparently were into Victorian antiques. Two stuffed wooden platform rockers stood on either end of the ancient couch Henry was sitting on. Each was covered with intricate lace doilies and antimacassars. In the corner of the room next to the south windows, stood a large bric-a-brac table filled with innocent little Hummel characters in carefree poses, chasing geese and running tiny spinning wheels. Looking at the quiet little sun-drenched characters, so lovingly and carefully arranged, gave Henry a strong tug of sadness. Were they destined to be packed up tomorrow and sent back east, never to be displayed again because of the unbearable memories they would recall?

Dill re-entered the room and sat in the rocker next to Henry.

"I wanted to get her permission before I told you this. We want to cooperate with any investigation but at the same time save the family—both families—any unnecessary grief. I hope I can speak to you in confidence."

"Well, to a certain degree," Henry said. "If your information is vital to obtaining a conviction of someone, I'd feel duty bound to share it."

"Yes. Only if it were necessary, you mean?"

"Yes."

"Very well, I'm sure that's Wilma's feeling too.

"We haven't been completely honest with you. There had been a marked change in Dr. Robinson, and Wilma just couldn't handle it. Poor kid, I've known her since she was a baby. Her daddy and my daddy were in the old negro baseball league together, with the old Chicago Hornets. When her folks found out about her problems, they got in touch with me in L.A. Anyway, once I determined how serious this was, I decided to try for an annulment."

"An annulment? Not a divorce?"

"Yes. Her folks are strict Catholics and she's been very sheltered. She really didn't know what she was getting into.

They'd been married less than a year. She'd been taken from her familiar surroundings and brought out here with a man she didn't know very well; a man who really misrepresented himself, you see. She was really married under false pretenses."

"How's that?" Henry asked.

"It's like this. Do you know the man hadn't so much as put his arms around her in over two months? Now I don't think Wilma is any sex maniac—in fact, I know she ain't. But that just ain't natural. She needs love and attention just like any other human being. And to be shut out and cast off by the man she loved was just more than she could take." Dill was having trouble keeping his voice down as his excitement rose.

"Did she ask him to obtain counseling?"

"She did; yes, she did, but he would have none of it. He said it was a problem that would work itself out. Obviously, it didn't."

"You mean their marriage has been . . . platonic?"

"No. I didn't say that, but since they moved out here, it's developed that way."

"You mean suddenly?"

"I mean since about two months ago. Anyway, in order to pursue the annulment angle, I needed some hard evidence of his playing around or something, so I had him followed."

"And you found out he was having an affair with his lab assistant."

Dill smiled. "You've been talking to Mrs. Ballard, haven't you? No, it wasn't Charlie. That's what Wilma thought, because he was spending so much time at the Center without any valid explanation. Mr. Garrott, Dr. Robinson has been consorting with a known homosexual." He rapped the armrest of the rocker for emphasis. "That's why he was so cool toward her. Those people develop a repugnancy toward the opposite sex—they don't even like to touch 'em."

Henry felt like laughing at Jimmy Dill's blanket charge of all homosexuals, but stifled his feelings. "Are you certain of this?"

"I sure am."

"When did you find this out?"

"About a week ago, I had him followed. He took the afternoon off and met his 'gentleman friend' in a restaurant. They had dinner together. Later that night, he was at the fellow's house. When Wilma asked him where he'd been, he said he was working."

"Maybe he was. He could have had business with him."

"Business, baloney. Everyone in town knows the guy is as queer as a three-dollar bill, and Robinson didn't even have his money in his bank."

Bells clanged in Henry's head; the image of Gilbert Lipert casually flopping his wrist and crying, "Oh, goodness! I know that," suddenly flashed before him.

"You mean it was a local banker he was having an affair with?"

"That's right. Mr. Lipert of the Almaden Commercial Bank. I had only funds for a three-day tail, but during those days they got together three times."

"Did you and Mrs. Robinson confront him with this information?"

"No, not yet—I mean, we didn't. It's not the kind of thing you just blurt out, you know. Once something like this is in the open, all the personal relationships change—the cat is out of the bag, so to speak. Besides, there's the family to think about. Robinson has a mother and two sisters back in Philadelphia who think the sun rises and sets on him. That's why we'd like to keep the whole thing quiet, if possible."

Henry, deep in thought, traced his index finger along the circular patterns in the armrest doily. "I find this kind of hard to believe."

"The way I figure it, is this," Dill offered, sliding forward in his rocker. "You say you're investigating a financial situation at the Center. I take it there are some funds missing?"

"Yes, there are."

"Of course; and this Lipert is a banker. He would know how to embezzle so there would be no incriminating evidence."

"Lipert and Robinson embezzling from the Center? But why?" Henry asked.

"Because they needed money to go away together; and if the police did start looking for them, Robinson would be passing for white by then, and the police would still be searching for a white and a black."

"As a matter of fact, the missing funds were in Lipert's bank."

"You see? You see? It all fits! It would be easy for him," Dill exclaimed.

"But that doesn't explain Robinson's death."

"Sure it does. They had a lover's quarrel. It often happens with those people; they're very insecure. My detective friend who was tailing them said they had an argument of some kind in the restaurant. Maybe the embezzling was getting out of hand, and Robinson wanted out; but Lipert wouldn't let him, you see. So, Robinson, who knew Lipert had been using the mail to defraud the Center, was using this to threaten him." He waved the letter from the Postal Inspector. "Lipert decided, if he couldn't have Robinson, nobody would. He lured him out to the Center on some pretext and killed him."

"And the fire at the Center?"

"Maybe Robinson told him he had hidden some evidence against Lipert as a safeguard, and Lipert decided to destroy it by fire."

"Hmmm. It's true, Lipert didn't have any love for the Center."

"You see? You see, it all fits," Dill whispered loudly.

But it didn't all fit. There was still the lab coat in Shoemaker's file drawer behind a locked door. And why, Henry wondered, would Robinson put on his own lab coat if he were meeting with Lipert? He would only put on a lab coat to work on a science project. Unless, of course, he only thought he was meeting with a fellow scientist. Perhaps he saw who he thought was his fellow scientist on the scaffold. Because he had received a forged note from Lipert arranging this meeting. When he ascended the scaffold, he found Lipert. An argument ensued, followed by a scuffle, and Robinson fell to his death.

It did satisfy another requirement, Henry determined. Robinson would know when people were away from the Center, so checks could be forged with relative safety. It would also explain why Robinson was snooping into Miss Matthews' travel records. He was looking for the name of someone who would be out of the area for a while. The Cleveland statement was just a cover.

Henry had seen almost every conceivable motive for people turning to spying, while he was in Europe, including homosexual drives. He could empathize with most of man's vices, but this was one he couldn't understand. Why anyone would want to give up a tall, slender, elegantly feminine beauty like Wilma, to go live with a middle-aged balding prig of a man, he would never know. He could only concede that such things did happen.

Unable to find any more fault with this theory, Henry encouraged Jimmy Dill to present his ideas to the police. They shook hands and Henry thanked him for his cooperation. He left his motel phone number and asked Dill to call if there were any new developments, then left.

Driving down the street toward Dr. Begelman's home, he thought about the similarity between this and the last case he was involved in in Europe. An older man marrying a younger woman—Robinson, around forty, considerably younger than his European counterpart, but apparently just as sneaky. The husband was deceiving the wife, the wife found out about it, "the cat was out of the bag," as Jimmy Dill would say, and dire consequences followed.

But Wilma didn't "let the cat out of the bag," according to Jimmy Dill. Maybe it made more sense that way. Maybe there wasn't any lover's quarrel. Maybe, after Jimmy Dill told her about Robinson, and Dill's fears about him leaving with a male lover, this so enraged Wilma she wanted revenge. She heard her husband planning to leave for the Center Saturday morning, or better yet, she faked a phone message from a co-worker that Robinson was urgently needed at the Center. She followed him there, knowing he would be climbing up a dangerous scaffolding and she climbed up after him. In a jealous rage, she killed him.

And Robinson's dying words, "Don't let 'um kill us"; could that "um" be interpeted as a "Wilma"? But there would be little danger of her killing anyone else—unless, of course, Robinson feared not for Henry but for his lover. The "us" could have meant Robinson and Lipert—"Don't let Wilma kill us."

Robinson's words were indelibly stamped on Henry's memory, and he ran them over and over, trying to get them to sound right. If Robinson didn't have enough lung power to sound out the word "Wilma," it could very well have come out as "um" to Henry's ears. And this would also explain why Robinson shook his head when Henry asked who was "trying to kill us." Henry had the wrong "us," and Robinson was trying to tell him so.

But the lab coat. That darn lab coat! She wouldn't put one on. It wouldn't hide her face or anything. And how did it get into Shoemaker's file drawer?

The Begelmans lived in a small, older cottage near the harbor in the old section of town. Henry drove slowly by and saw a woman with a large sunbonnet, industriously chopping away with a hoe in the midst of the flower garden, which occupied the entire front yard. The bonnet, the tall flowers, and the vine-covered latticework gate made Henry think of nursery rhymes: "Mary, Mary quite contrary, how does your garden grow?"

The street was crowded with old cars, pickups, and assorted trailers and rigs used in the harbor industries. He finally pulled into the parking lot of the Shrimp and Lobster Restaurant which was closed for remodeling, and walked toward the Begelman home.

So this was what had become of the great Fyodor Begelman. When Henry's high school chemistry teacher had breathlessly announced to her class the news of the new Nobel Award for Science, and the name of Fyodor Begelman was pronounced, Henry had imagined him to be in the never-never land of millionaires, presidents, kings and movie stars, where everyone is witty and clever, and dirt doesn't exist.

Even now, in his mature years when he should know better, he was still somehow surprised when he learned of some celebrity's clay feet. He had been raised in a climate similar to Miss Matthews', where certain ideas, and the people representing those ideas, were not challenged. While he had intellectually made the transition to the modern standard—suspicion of anything larger than the one-family farm—another part of him still gaped in awe at the old giants. He even thought his heart beat a little faster as he approached the woman with the hoe.

"Mrs. Begelman?" he asked at the garden gate.

The woman looked up without interrupting her short quick strokes. "Yes."

"I'm Mr. Garrott. I believe Mr. McCarthy's office called the other day saying I might be dropping by to see the Doctor."

"On Sunday?" She rested her hands on the end of the hoe handle, giving Henry a searching gaze, then reluctantly swung the gate open.

"Thanks," Henry said, and started past her.

Her firm hand on his chest stopped him.

"Wait here. I'll see if he can see you, Mr. Garrott." With the quick little gait of a busy housewife, she disappeared around the corner of the house. She apparently had a sun allergy, because in spite of the heat she wore long sleeves, gloves, and loose-fitting slacks—as well as the large bonnet.

The garden was a myriad of colors. Except for a few rows of vegetables, everything was flowers, and nearly everything was blooming. One plant, a groundcover succulent, with which Henry was not familiar, caught his eye. It had a bright blue flower and completely filled the borders of the entire garden, so that the overall effect was dazzling. He was about to pick a bud when Mrs. Begelman, without her bonnet, stepped out on the porch and invited him inside. Henry complimented her on her garden. She modestly attributed its entire success to the ocean air.

Henry stepped into a dark living room; he had to wait a moment for his eyes to adjust. Then he spotted the elderly gentleman clearing off a spot for his guest to sit. He was picking up newspapers and other loose pages from one end of an old leather sofa.

"Here; you can sit here, Mr. . . . ."

"Garrott. Henry Garrott, Dr. Begelman."

"Yes, yes," Begelman grunted, looking about for another spot to drop his armload. There wasn't a nearby spot, so he started toward his desk. He was noticeably dragging his left side, and the papers were held only with his good right arm. Finally, his wife came to his rescue and carried the papers into what used to be the dining room.

The first two rooms of the house had been turned over to the Doctor's work. Books lined most of the wall space; metal cabinets and cardboard boxes, jammed with dog-eared manila folders, filled much of the floor space of the old dining room.

"Sit, sit," Dr. Begelman insisted, as he lowered himself into his large desk chair. "Birdie, why don't we open some windows? I think Mr. . . . guest would like it cooler. We like it warm. We get like cold-blooded pack rats in our old age, eh?" He laughed and coughed at his own joke and then leaned against his old roll-top desk.

"Now then, what can I do for you?"

"I appreciate your taking the time to see me, Dr. Begelman."

He gestured a magnanimous "you're welcome" with every part of his upper body except the left forearm. "You say you're with the Center? What kind of—of—" He slapped a fist on his forehead.

"I'm helping Mr. McCarthy with the financial structure—"

"Work!" Begelman interrupted with a shout. "Work, work! Why can't I think of a simple word like that? You ever had a stroke Mr. . . .?"

"No, I haven't."

"Very interesting, the things that happen. The way the mind, the mind . . ."

". . . works," Henry interjected.

"Yes. Works. If I were younger, I would perform a study. Very interesting, the way of the mind.

"So, you are a money man, eh? Are you full time?"

"No, no, I'm only helping Mr. McCarthy temporarily. Dr. Begelman, I understand you are acting as the treasurer for the Center. Is that correct?"

"Treasurer for the . . .? Oh, yes. It was my turn."

"So you were paying the day-to-day bills, like the light bill, the heating. . . ."

Mrs. Begelman, who had been busy opening windows, came cautiously over and stood behind her husband's chair. Henry couldn't help but notice how much like a chicken she seemed in her manner and appearance. Her small hazel eyes blinked frequently, exposing white eyeball both above and below the hazel circles; her step was a thrust on one leg, then a pause on the other, so that it appeared she was casually scouring the living room for an elusive worm. Even her head would bob forward slightly on each thrust.

"No, Birdie would take care. . ." Begelman began without finishing.

"I wrote the checks out for things that were to be paid, such as supplies, and gardeners' fee; and the Doctor would sign them," Mrs. Begelman explained.

"So *you* actually kept the books?"

"Well, we just made out the checks when the bills came in."

"You didn't enter anything in the books?"

"We had three checkbooks for the three accounts: the Maintenance, the Equipment Supply, and the General Fund. We just wrote checks on the right accounts," Mrs. Begelman said. "That's the way we do our own accounts. Then we keep everything together and give it to the tax man at the end of the year, and he takes care of it."

"But how do you know how much your balance is? Aren't you afraid of being overdrawn?"

"Oh, the bank always calls and tells us when to put some more money in."

"I see . . ." Henry said, with a blank stare. "And the bank statements?"

"What's that?"

"Didn't you get a letter from the bank each month?"

"Oh, yes. We kept all those. Mr. McCarthy picked them up when he picked up the books last week. I think you'll find them all in order," Mrs. Begelman assured.

Begelman nodded and patted his wife's hand, underscoring the correctness of their procedures.

"Did you . . . you didn't check the bank statements against the checks you had written?"

Mrs. Begelman shook her head in unison with Henry's head.

"Why are you asking?" Mrs. Begelman wanted to know.

"Because it appears that at least $700,000 has been taken out of the General Fund by bogus—bad checks."

"Oh," Mrs. Begelman gasped. "But Mr. Garrott, isn't that against the law?"

"Yes, I strongly suspect that it might be," Henry said, trying to maintain the spirit of the interview.

"But they would have to have Bertha Corbut's signature on the checks," Begelman said. "Even I did."

"Yes, I know. It appears they forged that too."

"But they can't do that. She should be told."

Mrs. Begelman patted his shoulder. "He forgets. He knows she's dead, but he forgets."

"Oh, yes, poor Bertha. I should have gone to the meeting."

Mrs. Begelman pulled a large handkerchief from the breast pocket of her husband's tweed jacket, and held it ready for the tears she knew would fall.

"Let's not talk about Bertha now," she said, patting his shoulder.

"But I could have gone. I wasn't that sick, but you said I should stay in bed," he whined.

"Darling, listen; you had a high fever. You couldn't go."

"Yes, I should have gone . . . meeting."

Mrs. Begelman wiped his left eye and the corner of his mouth, almost without looking, and appealed to Henry for understanding. "We had a bad experience at the Center a few months back and it preys upon his mind."

She began pumping his left arm and hand in an exercise pattern, as though she could jerk his mind onto another subject. "Let's think about something else now, shall we? We haven't done our afternoon exercises yet, dear."

He jerked his left arm away from her with his right arm. "We, we, we. Don't use plurals on me!"

"All right now, all right." She took his left arm back and gently continued with the hand exercises. "Mr. Garrott is here about the finances, the finances at the Center."

"Yes, yes, I know . . . I'm not a child."

But she had successfully manipulated his mind away from the death of Bertha Corbut, just as one would that of a child. Henry wanted to pursue Begelman's relationships with the other members of the General Fund Committee, but realized it would probably lead the old man into the same reaction of remorse and guilt, so he decided to stay clear of the subject.

"Dr. Begelman, I understand you were influential in getting Dr. Robinson on the staff."

"Yes. Dr. Robinson. He is a good man."

"*Is* a good man? Did you know about—" Henry caught sight of Mrs. Begelman's blinking eyes and realized the doctor had not been told of Robinson's death. He cleared his throat and continued, "Could you tell me something of his work?"

"You are a money man, not a scientist, correct?"

Henry nodded.

"All right, then. He works on an important genetic disease which affects the black people."

"Yes, sickle-cell anemia."

"Oh, you know. Then what more is there to say?"

"I understand his research was progressing badly. Would you know anything about that?"

"That is the nature of research. You have many bad days . . . only a few good days, but ahhh, the good days are worth the waiting, eh, Birdie?"

She added an extra pat in her hand manipulation to let him know she agreed.

"But he did look up to you for guidance and direction. I thought perhaps he had confided in you about his prob—"

"Ha! Confided? He is a pest. I send him away but he comes back . . ."

"Now now," Birdie clucked, trying to calm him.

"I tell him a new detection system will not . . . is no good. So what—you detect easy who has sickle cells? You can't ask millions of young people not to make their babies. The answer to the problem lies in the chromosomes, in the DNA. We've got to weed out the bad dots; find the ones that carry sickle cell and weed out. Break into the code."

"And he wouldn't take your advice?" Henry asked.

"Oh, he would nod and say, 'Yes, yes,' and the next week he was back asking, 'How do you recognize this part? How does this look on the scope when it is defective?' "

"In other words, he was back working on a detection system instead of—"

"Yes. Workin' on a detection system. I try to help the young men, but if they won't take your advice, what can you. . ." He shrugged.

"Yes, I see," Henry assured. "Tell me, was Dr. Robinson

working on anything that might have made him impotent?"

"Impotent? You mean with the sex? No. I been fifty-three years with the genes and I still got—"

Birdie halted him with an extra hard tug. "He doesn't want to know about you," she scolded.

"That hurts," he growled.

"Well, then talk right."

"I do talk right. He asks if Dr. Robinson is impotent, and I say no. Sterile, maybe, but impotent, no."

"Sterile?"

"Sure. Virus or bacteria can make you sterile. Did you ever hear of a grown man with the mumps? Very bad, very bad."

"Could he . . . do you think there is a possibility he was working with viruses that rendered him—"

"No, no. He was not using viruses. That I know. Besides, no scientist at the Center is permitted to ex . . . ah . . . word . . ."

Birdie helped out with "experiment."

"Yes, experiment on himself. Very bad; we all sign pledges—no self-testing. That was a rule from old General Kilbourne."

"What would happen to him if he did test something on himself and they found out about it?"

"He could be dis . . . ah . . . go, let go. But he is not yet on the testing level. He has miles to go . . . just opening the door. He has nothing to test."

He muttered gruffly to Birdie, "Enough. That's enough now with the hand. You wear me down."

"Can you tell me a little bit more about what you wanted him to work on? About breaking into the genetic code, somehow and—"

"All right, I make it easy for you." He held up his right hand. "Here we make the sperm from the male with its own DNA code, and over here . . ."

Birdie helped him raise his left hand.

". . . we have the egg of the female and code. Now many carry sickle-cell genes but don't have the disease. Must be dominant to make disease. Now let us say these hands have genes that will make disease in baby. They come together." He banged his right hand against his left, then forced them quickly apart. They don't stay together. They don't mix—like horse and mule. No match. That is what we work on."

Birdie reacted, "You said 'work.' "

"What?"

"You said 'work.' "

"Yes, I did . . . it is going to be a good day."

"Doctor, this sounds a great deal like what Professor Ballard is working on," Henry said.

"In principle, yes. Shoemaker, too, and many many others have the dream to improve the code through . . . through . . ." He searched.

"Manipulation?" Henry attempted.

"Yes, outside manipulation. That is better than what I was looking to use."

"But isn't that terribly risky? I mean, you're talking about influencing human life."

Birdie rose from her husband's side and started her strange pacing behind his chair as Begelman waxed philosophical.

"You must remember Mr. . . . young man, there are people crippled and dying every day because of the bad genes they came into this world with. Are we to wash our hands and say, 'too bad'? What kind of humanity is this? Man has a brain, and each day he knows more and more. We will break through. We will."

"And what happens when you make a mistake? Will you kill the monsters you create, or will you—"

"Monsters. What kind of nonsense?"

"We seem to learn more and more, as you say. But the spirit of man doesn't seem to keep pace."

"Excuse me, Mr. Garrott," Birdie interrupted, "but what does all this have to do with the finances of the Center?"

"Yes, you're right," Henry confessed. "I am getting a bit far afield, aren't I? Thanks so much for your time," he said, rising.

"No, no, wait. Look here, look," Begelman insisted, and searched his desk cubicles until he came across a small framed picture. Thrusting it at Henry, he demanded, "Look at this, will you?"

It was an old black and white snapshot of Begelman and a spry David Ben-Gurion planting a small tree in front of a group of shirt-sleeved dignitaries.

"Twenty-two years ago Mr. . . . we planted that tree. You see me there with the Prime Minister of Israel. And yesterday we received a letter from our grandson. He ate his lunch in the shade of that same tree, he wrote us."

"Yes, very nice."

"You don't understand, do you? That is my philosophy! We build for the future. It is good to have trees in the world. Good, not bad. And we build with spirit, and with brains, for the future. That is what I believe in!" Begelman shouted angrily.

Henry had a distinct feeling he and Begelman had lost their communication link. He seemed to be refuting an argument Henry had not presented. Mrs. Begelman helped her husband rise, and Henry made a graceless farewell.

Out in the garden, he lingered over the flowers a moment, then heard the front door behind him reopen. Birdie came out and down the steps, while adjusting her bonnet.

"Mr. Garrott, one minute." She took her small clippers out of her pocket, snipped several cuttings of the border flowers, and wrapped them in a wet paper towel she had brought with her.

"Here. I saw you looking at these before."

He protested because of his distance from home, but she assured him they were hardy blossoms, and if he kept the stems moist, they would last until he could plant them.

"Thank you for not telling my husband about Dr. Robinson. I simply couldn't tell him. It would just upset him so, and as it is, he only has a few good hours a day—and the book has to come first. It just has to."

"I hope I didn't upset him with my comments at the end."

"Oh, no, no. His temper is like that now, since the stroke. It isn't really him. He never used to raise his voice. It comes on him at the strangest times, too."

"Mrs. Begelman, could you tell me anything more about Dr. Robinson? He had been acting quite strangely the last month or so, and I can't seem to get an angle on what it was all about."

"We wouldn't know much about that. We didn't see much of them socially. We didn't have all that much in common. Oh, it wasn't a race problem, I assure you. Mrs. Robinson, the wife, didn't seem to care much for the kind of talk scientists get into, and I think it disturbed Gregory to see his wife so ill at ease. There was quite a difference in their ages, you know."

"Yes, I know."

"And then when Fyodor had his stroke, we stopped going out, and had to convert our cottage into his study so he could continue his work. No more clam chowder get-togethers with the staff. I truly miss those times together."

"When was the last time you saw Dr. Robinson?"

"Let me see . . . I think it was last Thursday. Yes. That's the day I cut back the begonias. Not the right time of the year, but they were crowding the—"

"Were you with the men when they talked?"

She moved around to get her back to the sun. "Oh, I think I was in and out. I don't pay much attention when they start spouting all their technical terms."

"Did Dr. Robinson bring papers over here to work on or—"

"Just a light briefcase, as I recall."

"But it was a work session, and not just a social call?"

"Yes. I was going to ask him to stay for lunch, but they didn't work that long."

"And you don't know what they talked about?" Henry asked, looking off toward the house.

"Mr. Garrott, please. We have already told you everything we know about Dr. Robinson." She gestured as if to escort him out of the yard. "If we can think of anything, we'll let you know. The Doctor doesn't have very much time left; I know that. There's no point in deceiving ourselves, and we have to do away with the distractions."

"I understand. The book comes first."

"Yes. The book comes first."

Henry rolled down the windows of his sun-baked car and cruised around the waterfront on the streets adjacent to the Begelman's home. Most of the other homes were in various stages of dilapidation, landscaped with weeds and junk cars. A few blocks away was the small local cannery. Even on the weekend, the smell was pretty gamey. When the wind was right, the aroma would certainly reach the Begelmans'. Was this atmosphere conducive to the development of world-moving books? Henry longed for a look at their financial statement.

At the local jail Henry found out the prisoner A. K. Shoemaker was being held at the county jail north of town. By the time he arrived at the county complex, word of his interest in Shoemaker must have been called ahead, because Henry was ushered into an interview room as soon as he made himself known. He was soon joined by one of the arresting officers he had seen in the restaurant. He introduced himself as Deputy Sheriff Tugwell and settled in as though he was going to be there for some time.

"What did you want to see the prisoner about?"

"I'm temporarily working at the Kilbourne Center and need to get some information from him," Henry said.

"What kind of information?"

Henry was getting tired of saying it. He heaved a sigh and began:

"I'm working on the financial situation of the Center, and Mr. Shoemaker was serving on one of the finance committees. I'd like to ask him some questions about his involvement."

"On the committee?"

"Yes."

"And nothing more?"

"Why? Am I limited to what I can talk to him about?"

Tugwell smiled. "You know we don't have to let you see him. He's not to be arraigned until tomorrow morning, and we can keep everybody away from him except his lawyer—if we want to."

"I see. Are you saying I can't see him?"

Tugwell drummed his fingers on the tabletop in an annoying manner—no doubt a device he used during interrogations. He smiled and watched Henry. "You wouldn't be thinking about changing your story, would you?"

Henry wished he could kick himself for his own stupidity. This was the first time he fully realized he was the the State's star witness in the case. He knew it, and yet he didn't know it. He had given his information about the accident twice the day before, but because he was so used to briefing and debriefing sessions in his government work, the fact he was to be called as a witness at a trial had not sunk in. Testimony for him had only been so much information to be gathered and used.

What if he had misunderstood what Robinson had said? Since it didn't make all that much sense, perhaps he did miss his meaning. Until now, Henry had been excited about his work—even enjoying it, if that was the right word. Now the enormity of his responsibility finally reached him. At best, his testimony was destined to ruin the effectiveness of Shoemaker's career; at worst, a lengthy prison term.

"I will tell what I heard and saw," Henry stated gravely, "and what I heard and saw is what I've already told the other officers."

Tugwell was eyeing his face carefully, and grinning, which made Henry wonder how many of his own thoughts he was telegraphing.

"What are you charging him with?"

"Murder two," Tugwell said flatly, without changing expression.

"I see. That's—"

"We figure it's good for about two years. His lawyer is a flake. We could go for murder one, but with his status and clean background, I doubt we could make it hold up."

Tugwell's smile was very disturbing to Henry.

"Don't worry, pal. Just do your civic duty and everything."

"Thank you, Deputy," Henry assured. "I understand my duties. May I see him now?"

Tugwell rose. "Okay. I'll have to put an officer in with you, though." He opened the door for Henry, and walked beside him down the corridor.

"By the way, we found traces of the broken balls embedded in his shoe soles. He'd been scuffing around for half an hour or so out on the road, but we still found 'em. Just thought you'd like to know." Tugwell smiled a little more broadly.

"So that puts him at the scene?"

"What else?"

Henry didn't bother to tell him Saturday was not the first time plastic orbs had been broken in Shoemaker's presence. The more airtight Tugwell felt his case against Shoemaker was, the better chance Henry would have of getting a good interview with the prisoner. Strange, how easily he slipped into an advisory role with the police.

Going down the labyrinth of corridors, they passed a large open area, and Henry caught a glimpse of the young lady with the large glasses he had seen the first day at the Center. She was being hurried down another corridor, in the opposite direction, by a uniformed policewoman.

"Hey, wasn't that . . . was that Charlie—"

"Yes, it was."

"I'd like to speak with her, if I may. Would you excuse—"

"Not now, Garrott. She's here to make a statement."

Tugwell took Henry's arm and made one last turn halting at a door covered with steel bars. "Wait here," he ordered, pushing a button on the wall and disappearing back down the hallway.

A uniformed woman opened the door and directed him into a large room with tables for lawyers and their clients. Shoemaker was on his way, she affirmed, and for fifteen cents she would be happy to get him a cup of coffee while he waited. In a few minutes, the coffee arrived, and the woman took her position on a high chair in the middle of the room, as though she were about to judge a tennis match.

Henry took out his pocket date book and tried to jot down the questions he wanted to ask. It was more to keep him busy while he waited. The thought of being behind bars again didn't do much for his nervous system.

Finally the prisoner was escorted in. Shoemaker looked surprisingly good. The loose-fitting jail denims hid his bulk quite well, and except for a slight hollow look around his eyes, he seemed to be bearing up.

"What have you found out?" he asked excitedly as he sat

down opposite Henry.

"You're to speak in a full voice," the policewoman reminded them, "so I can hear everything that's said."

"To tell you the truth, not very much."

Shoemaker's face fell. "But I thought—when I heard you were here—you had something. You got my note, didn't you?"

Henry nodded. "Did you know there was a fire at the Center this morning?"

"Fire? Was anything destroyed?"

"Some files Ballard shared with Robinson," Henry began, while watching Shoemaker's reactions to the events. He wanted to know all the details of the fire, and gave the impression he didn't know Robinson had stored materials in the bottom drawer of the file in Ballard's office.

Henry changed the subject by asking, "Listen. In your note you said you suspected Mrs. Begelman. Why did you say that?"

"Oh, I don't know. It's a crazy idea."

"She's got to be pushing seventy, you know."

"I realize that. Here's all I know. My cleaning lady lives across the street from them, and last Friday she gave me an earful about a squabble at the Begelman house. She was bringing in her groceries, from her car, and she heard raised voices from Begelmans' living room. She then saw Begelman pushing a light-skinned negro out of the front door, with lots of shouting going on."

"No doubt Robinson. He was there on Thursday, according to Mrs. Begelman," Henry added.

"And when he jumped back up the steps to continue arguing with the old man, Mrs. Begelman, who had been working in the garden, chased him out of the yard with her hoe."

"She raised her hoe at Robinson?"

"According to Mrs. Ramirez—and I don't know why she would lie about a thing like that."

"Did she hear anything that was actually said?"

"She heard the black say something like, 'Somebody's been leading me down the garden path and I'm going to find out who it is.' Then Mrs. Begelman yelled, 'I'll lead *you* down the garden path,' and proceeded to *literally* chase him through the garden and out of their yard."

"Weird," Henry chuckled, and eyed the policewoman who was trying not to appear interested.

He could easily see Dr. Begelman losing his temper, raising his voice, and perhaps chasing someone out of his house. Henry had gotten a taste of his wrath himself. But Mrs. Begelman? She had impressed Henry as a bit high strung, but she was most certainly rational and reasonable.

He asked again, "You mean she actually raised her hoe and threatened him?"

"That's what she said," Shoemaker assured. "And she seemed certain about the black saying the 'garden path' line, because she thought it funny when he literally was chased down the path."

"Do you have any idea why Mrs. Begelman would do such a thing?"

"Sure. She's very protective of her husband's time. Robinson was probably challenging some of his pet theories, and she knew her husband would be ruined for any writing the rest of the day if the argument went any further."

"It's a strange incident, but I can't see how it applies—"

"You mean you can't see her climbing up the scaffold and pushing Robinson off?" Shoemaker turned to the policewoman: "I hope you're getting all this."

"Every word," she muttered, straight-faced.

"Fine, because there'll be a ten-point quiz, first thing Monday morning, and it will bear heavily on your making sergeant before the next snowfall."

"Very funny."

"I thought so."

Henry interrupted, "This hoe thing hardly is the basis for a motive to murder."

"But it does show she's capable of violence."

"Capable of *threatening* violence."

"Okay, okay. But let me just bounce this off you: Robinson has been following Dr. Begelman's work, reading everything he can get his hands on; then he finds what he feels is an error in Begelman's calculations and confronts Begelman with it. Begelman sees there might be some validity to the charge, but can't face the possibility because it would wash out a lifetime of work. Rather than encourage criticism, like a good scientist should, he decides to stonewall it. Then his wife sees what is going on, and in an effort to protect her husband's career, reputation, and whatever, she helps out with a little 'push' in the right direction." Shoemaker sits back, watching Henry's face to see how his idea landed.

Henry twisted his lips and shook his head. "I don't buy it."

"Would it help if I told you this is precisely what has happened to Begelman's work? Now, don't misunderstand me. I don't mean to disparage the man. He's a giant. When the layman thinks of genetics today, he still thinks of Begelman. His early work was truly important, but time marches on, and new techniques and tools have contradicted most of his old pet theories.

"It's no disgrace; it's just the way life is," Shoemaker continued. "We take three steps forward and two steps back. The same thing happened to Freud. We revere him as the Father of modern psychiatry in spite of the fact that virtually every one of his theories is now in disfavor. Some of us can adjust to reality better than others, but once you've been in the spotlight for so long, it's pretty difficult to sit on the bench. Begelman just can't seem to make the switch. He's like a great composer who gave the world a new and innovative musical style, but now here he is, still playing the same old tune, while the world is clamoring after a new composer.

"I can tell you what's going to happen with this book he's struggling to finish. He'll get it published because of his name, but then it will sit on shelves collecting dust, because it will be a rehash of all his old theories, with a few lame arguments thrown in for support. He's on staff here because the Center needs a Nobel Prize winner, but he hasn't laid any golden eggs since he was thirty-five years old. We all know that—all except Robinson—and we just work around him."

"That's all very enlightening, but it still doesn't explain what happened on the scaffold."

"Sure it does. That whole DNA model was his idea—his and his wife's. It's supposed to be the most definitive structure of its kind; built primarily for publicity actually, but it started growing in importance when the different elements started going into place, and everyone walking by had their own opinion about its development. The damn thing is so visual. I wish we'd never started it, but Begelman threatened to quit if we didn't build it.

"Anyway, Mrs. Begelman has been taking a very active role in it, especially since the doctor's stroke."

"She's been on the scaffold before?"

"I haven't actually seen her on the scaffold, but she's most certainly capable of getting up there."

"And you think Robinson got up early Saturday morning, put on his lab coat, and climbed the scaffold to talk with a nonscientist?"

"Well, it's a possibility," he shrugged. "She could have been carrying a vital message, or explanation, supposedly. Anything to entice him up there."

"And then she cold-bloodedly proceeded to push him off." Henry wagged his head. "I think we can drop that line of thought. Little old ladies just don't act that way."

"All right, maybe it was an accident. Maybe she—" He gave up and looked down at his hands. "I know I'm grasping at straws—I can't think straight in here. I'll have bail set tomorrow after the arraignment and I'll be out of here. This has been quite an experience, you know that?"

"Yes, I'm sure it has."

Shoemaker pulled out his first cigarette and lit up.

"So Begelman threatened to quit, did he?" Henry asked. "Are they pretty well off?"

Shoemaker shrugged, "They vacation in Europe and Israel whenever they've a mind to. That's about all I know. Why?"

"I was wondering why they live in that little two-by-four house down by the water."

"He's under a doctor's care, you know. I think he's supposed to walk and get plenty of sea air. They're not the kind who go in for prestigious addresses, anyway."

"No, I suppose not." Henry backed his chair up and leaned back to get away from the nicotine fog spreading toward him. "Let's get back to Robinson and his project. Tell me anything you can think of about him—especially the last two months."

"I told you before. I think he was in over his head. He was a very ineffective researcher." Shoemaker shrugged.

"You seem to hold your colleagues in very low esteem."

"I do, don't I? I'm a realist. There really aren't that many smart people in the world, and you have to be smart to do effective research."

"If Robinson had been white, would that have made him any more intelligent in your eyes?"

Shoemaker looked out the high windows at the sky and exhaled heavily. "Oh, brother. Nice day outside, is it?"

"You might as well get used to it. You're going to get plenty of that line if this thing goes to trial."

"Yes, you're right, of course. The answer to your question is no. He would have been just as ineffective if he'd been lily white."

"All right now, let me do a little supposing. Suppose Robinson was a good researcher. He set up his programs in an orderly, scholarly fashion and his work was proceeding slowly, but progress was being made. Then about two months ago something happened—something which demanded increasingly larger blocks of his time, until his own research work was being neglected.

"This something preyed upon his mind. He knew a little bit, but he had to know more. He pestered Begelman, Shoemaker, Ballard, anyone who would listen, until he got the information he needed. But then, once he had this information, he confronted someone with it and was killed for his efforts. Then the killer, in an effort to erase all trace of this secret, destroyed Robinson's records."

"Yes, yes," Shoemaker enthused, blinking his eyes rapidly and hard. He lit up another cigarette without bothering to extinguish the smoldering one in the ash tray.

"Please, just one at a time. Okay?"

"Oh, sorry," he said, crushing the butt. "Part of it makes sense. I was impressed with the way he got things going; 'Great beginning, lousy ending,' I remember thinking. But what was this something he was supposed to know?"

"That's what I'm hoping you'll tell me. You're the scientist."

Shoemaker ran his fingers through his heavy, wavy hair, as

though he were searching for a trace of an idea.

"It no doubt involved money. There have been funds misappropriated," Henry offered, "but I've a feeling it's a good deal more than that. Otherwise why would he have been pestering you for information?"

"But why didn't he come right out and say what was on his mind? Why didn't he make a public accusation about whatever it was? If this, this thing, had been festering inside his brain for two months, why did he keep such deep, dark secrets? Surely after two months he could have found somebody he could trust with this information."

"I know, I know." Henry conceded. "And it could have been a combination of things—something in his personal life, plus something. Do you think he was a homosexual?"

Shoemaker raised his eyebrows and snapped his head back. "What a stupid question! What has that got to do with anything?"

"Do you?"

"I haven't the foggiest notion. Don't let your literal interpretation of the Bible hinder your ability to think objectively."

"Maybe we're both jumping to conclusions," Henry argued, to change the subject. "What are your feelings now about Dr. Jones? She's convinced *you* were the one who killed their program."

Shoemaker leaned back in his chair and looked at Henry with pure disgust. "Look, this isn't getting us anywhere. I told you what I . . . how I voted. I don't need this harassment. I thought you were coming over here with some answers."

Henry had a sinking feeling in the pit of his stomach; it said he was losing the confidence of the one person who held the key to the whole problem. He'd handled it poorly. Shoemaker was closer to the raw edge than he thought, and this floundering accountant, playing detective, was just one more pointless grilling he could do without.

Shoemaker fussed again about being surrounded by people with small minds, and stormed out of the room. The exit reminded Henry of a chubby little boy running home to Mommy where his true talents would be appreciated. He felt sorry for A. K. Shoemaker when he thought of what a sharp District

Attorney would do with his haughty airs, brilliant mind, and rotund body. He had so many traits the man in the street, or the jury, would find offensive that a conviction would not be hard to come by. Now, when he needed friends, he had become his own worst enemy.

As he searched for the elusive hallway which would lead him out of the building, Deputy Sheriff Tugwell mysteriously appeared at Henry's elbow.

"Did you two have a nice chat?"

"No. It was extremely unproductive," Henry confided.

"You don't seem to think he's guilty, do you?"

Henry didn't respond so he went on. "Mind telling me why?" He gestured toward a room full of small office cubicles with desks and chairs. "Come on, sit down. My office is right in here." They moved in, sat, and Tugwell offered refreshments in a friendly manner, which Henry refused coolly. But he did proceed to tell Tugwell of pressing his ear to the door at the entrance of the Center Saturday morning, and of hearing what sounded like a lighter person coming down the scaffold.

Tugwell's only response was a scowl, as he broke up the sugar cubes in his coffee.

"Anything else?"

"Nnoo, nothing specific. There was the comment Shoemaker made when you arrested him in the restaurant."

"What comment was that?"

"When you told him about finding the lab coat in the lower drawer, he didn't act like a guilty man."

"How's a guilty man supposed to act?"

"If you'll recall, you didn't mention anything about the torn pocket. Now, if he'd known about the torn pocket, he would have said something about your right to search his office or wanting a lawyer before he said anything else. He would probably have said anything other than what he did."

"And you remember what it was he said?"

"Yes, don't you?"

Tugwell smiled. This time the smile seemed a bit more genuine. "No, I'm afraid I don't."

"He said, 'But I always hang up my lab coat behind my door.'"

"And that told you he was innocent?"

"It sounds to me like the remark of a person who knew nothing of the torn pocket."

Tugwell snorted, "Boy, have you got a lot to learn about human nature. We're dealing here with a highly intelligent guy. Of course he'd pretend not to know about the torn pocket."

"Then there's the matter of the wrong-size lab coat. It was a medium, but Shoemaker wore a—"

"He could fit into it, he could fit into it. They don't generally button those things anyway."

"Now, think for a minute. Robinson has just been pushed. While losing his balance, he turns and makes one desperate swipe at his assailant to regain his balance. If it had been Shoemaker, I think he would have grabbed for his shirt pocket or his jacket or his eyeglasses. I just can't see him hitting the small lab coat which would probably be bunched up around Shoemaker's armpits."

"He made a lucky hit," Tugwell shrugged.

Henry sat back. Tugwell continued, "I don't know why you're so anxious to prove him innocent. If he didn't do it, there's only one other person we can prove was at the scene of the crime." Tugwell pursed his lips and raised his eyebrows to Henry.

"Oh. Have you come up with a motive for that other person yet?"

"No, we haven't felt the need to do so—yet."

Henry moved about, re-crossing his legs. Tugwell laughed, then rose from his chair and stretched his head over the partition wall behind him. "Timmy, you got that copy for me yet?"

"Right here," the unseen Timmy replied from behind the partition. Tugwell reached over to retrieve a cassette tape.

"Now, it's my turn," Tugwell announced, dropping the tape into the cassette player on the back corner of his desk. It was the voice of Charlie Bell giving her name, date, and the purpose of the interview.

"I'll roll it to the good stuff," the officer said, and put the machine on fast forward until it neared the spot he was looking for.

Tugwell: When was this?

Charlie: Friday morning.

Tugwell: How can you be so sure it was—

Charlie: Because Fridays were Professor Shoemaker's days to work on the DNA model. They have to take turns, because it's so hard to move the scaffold platform.

Tugwell: Okay, it was Friday.

Charlie: Anyway, he came back into the supply room.

Tugwell: Now, who did? Please use names and not pronouns.

Charlie: Dr. Robinson, of course. Isn't that who I'm talking about?

Tugwell: You're absolutely right. Go ahead. Dr. Robinson came back into the supply room.

Charlie: And he said he'd been arguing with Professor Shoemaker. He seemed very upset.

Tugwell: About what?

Charlie: They'd broken one of their elements—they're very expensive to replace. He and, uh, I mean Dr. Robinson and Shoemaker had been arguing over the placement of an element that affects skin pigmentation. Shoemaker had grabbed it out of his hands, and it fell and broke.

Tugwell: Was it at this time Dr. Robinson made the statement about his feeling Professor Shoemaker was not being truthful with him about the elements?

Charlie: Nnno, that came later. Friday afternoon.

Tugwell: Do you know what made him come to that conclusion?

Charlie: I'm not sure, but I did see him talking with Professor Ballard in his office—Professor Ballard's office—most of the afternoon.

Tugwell: Did anyone else see them in there together?

Charlie: Well, anyone in the main lab could look right in the windows and see them.

Tugwell: Did Professor Shoemaker see them in there?

Charlie: He was in the lab part of that time, so I suppose he did.

Tugwell: All right, now, tell us exactly what happened.

Charlie: Well, about 3:30, or a quarter to four, I went into Dr. Robinson's office with the news that a lot of his cultures had spoiled. I told him I would have to throw them away. He didn't seem to be concerned about it at all, in spite of the fact it represented about four months of hard work on my part—well, both our parts. I was quite upset, to say the least. But he just said he could start on those cultures later— that right now time was of the essence. He'd found out who had been lying to him, and he was going to have it out with him.

Tugwell: And who did he say had been lying to him?

Charlie: I asked him directly, and he said Shoemaker.

Tugwell: And did he say when he was going to confront Shoemaker?

Tugwell clicked the recorder off and smiled across at Henry. "What do you think of your Mr. Shoemaker's innocence now?"

"What was her answer to that last question?"

"She didn't know when he planned to meet him. But, since he said time was of the essence, it no doubt meant they would meet Saturday morning."

"Why didn't they meet Friday evening or that afternoon? It was only 4 p.m."

"Who knows? Maybe he couldn't reach Shoemaker."

"So you can't definitely prove they had an early morning appointment?"

"You're kind of hard to convince, aren't you?"

"I would say Shoemaker would be very unlikely to come to the Center on a Saturday morning just to continue an argument with someone he considered his scholastic inferior."

"Ah, but he did come to the Center." Tugwell rapped his desk.

"This could go on forever. What are you going to do now?"

"I'm going over to see this Ballard guy. See if we can find out what it was Shoemaker was lying about."

"May I tag along?"

"Afraid not. Against department policy." He rose, "C'mon, we're locking up this section of the building. I'll let you out our side entrance."

As they walked, Tugwell reminded him of the procedure of American courts. Henry would be needed for the pretrial hearing, and the District Attorney would probably push for an early date. Henry was to inform him if he needed to leave town. Henry asked for a phone number where he could reach Tugwell; he wanted to talk with the detective after he'd talked to Ballard, he explained.

Tugwell smiled, "Still in there pitchin', aren't you?" He unlocked the side door. "We'll be in touch."

Henry found himself in the parking lot a few yards away from his car. The evening sun was settling somewhere behind the hazy clouds that were hanging over the colorless ocean and it had turned cool. A shiver went up Henry's back, and he suddenly felt very lonely. He hadn't eaten since morning and decided he'd feel better with some hot food inside him. He'd pick up something, go back to the motel, and call Valery. That's what he needed. Weekends in strange small towns were the pits the world over.

He found a Fish and Chips take-out restaurant that specialized in fresh local catches, and decided to try it.

There were two messages waiting at the motel desk: McCarthy had called three times and Jimmy Dill had called with an urgent message for him to call back. Henry decided to eat while the food was still semi-warm. He made himself comfortable on the bed, picnic style, and offered a quick prayer of thanks. The fish was excellent. His spirits seemed to revive with every bite and he downed his food quickly, as was his custom.

Contented, he stretched out, laced his hands behind his neck, and tried to mull over what he had learned thus far. Mozart, it was said, created his greatest works "without effort" while taking a carriage ride after an enjoyable meal. Perhaps the same principle would hold true for creative deduction.

One technique his group in Europe had found helpful in smoking out a double agent involved filing all the information about an event into a computer by source. This way if one of their sources was lying, this fact would often surface when the event was reconstructed by the computer without the input of the phony source. Conversely, the information about an event would invariably make less sense with the faulty information left in.

Assuming someone had been lying to him, he tried to play the computer game in his mind, but quickly remembered he was not the only person who had been lied to. Robinson. And that meant the only words or actions of Robinson's that could be relied upon would be what he did or said *after* he found out he'd been lied to.

Now, what were some of these post-lie things? He said, "Time was of the essence"—he got up early Saturday morning—he had invited Henry to meet him at the Center on the spur of the moment. This did not impress Henry as being in keeping with his earlier actions of near desperation. Why would he allow four months of work to go down the drain because of major distractions one moment and then casually tell Henry to drop by on him at work the next morning? Henry's health problem may have been critical, that's true, but why didn't Robinson simply steer him to the emergency ward of the hospital instead of volunteering his own services? Was his time problem a thing of the past at that point? "Time is of the essence"—Henry ran the words over in his mind until they started to become meaningless.

He rubbed his eyes vigorously. Just more questions, and still no answers. Mozart, he decided, had his own unique system; Henry had yet to find his.

He dialed the Robinson residence and learned from the somber-voiced Wilma that Jimmy Dill was on his way back to Los Angeles. The reason he had called, she explained, was because they had found the remnants of a letter her husband had started.

"We found it tor' up in the bottom of the wastebasket in

his study. I don't remember when I emptied the basket last, so I don't know how long it's been there. Prob'ly two weeks since I emptied it. He hardly ever has stuff in there, so I don't bother to empty it."

She sounded as though she could go on forever with minor details, but Henry finally steered her around to reading the message. She began matter-of-factly:

" 'My Dearest Darling Wilma,
    It has never been my desire to hurt you in any way. You know that. And it is now with a terribly heavy heart that I ask you to release me from our marriage vows.
    It is because you are so young, my darling, that I . . . ,'

That's as far as it goes," she said.

"I see . . . and there's no date?"

"No."

"Well, I'm very sorry. This seems to strengthen what you and Mr. Dill suspected all along, doesn't it?"

"Yes, it does," she said. For the first time her voice seemed to be losing its coolness. "We found it tor' up in three pieces. It was just crumpled up in the bottom of the wastebasket in his study. I didn't even know it was . . ." She couldn't finish.

Henry tried to think of a sober, logical question he could ask to help get her mind off her problems, but couldn't come up with one. He asked if there was anything he could do to help.

"My mother is gonna come out tomorrow. She's gonna fly out and Jimmy will bring her up to be with me.

"Jimmy just thought you o'tta know."

"Yes, thank you. I'm glad you told me. Now, don't hesitate to call if I can help, okay?"

"Thank you. Bye."

Henry hung up and immediately regretted the cheeriness in his voice. What do you say to grieving people? He still remembered, with resentment, the strange things well-intentioned people had said to him when his own mother died. Even the Christians with their talk of the life hereafter because of the

Resurrection meant little to a grieving boy. The same talk coming from a white stranger would no doubt have a similar effect on Wilma. About the only thing one could do, he decided, was to let the person know of your own sense of loss. Since he didn't really know Gregory Robinson, that would be inappropriate.

Henry tried to ring his home phone for the second time, but still no one answered. They may have gone out for dinner, he thought.

Well, he'd stalled as long as he could. He dialed McCarthy's number. Millie answered, slipping into a cool, reserved tone of voice as soon as she recognized Henry's voice.

"Where have you been? Vernon has been calling all over trying to reach you."

"I'm sorry. I've been out most of the day. Say, I wanted to tell you what an outstanding dinner that was Friday evening. I want to thank—"

"Yes, yes. You're more than welcome. Vernon has had to rush into Los Angeles. The director of his grant committee—you know, the government grant?"

"Yes, I certainly do."

"The chairman is flying to the Orient, and had a layover in Los Angeles, so he wanted to see Vernon personally. He phoned—"

"That sounds encouraging, doesn't it?" Henry said.

"Mr. Garrott, he asked me to tell you not to do or say anything more about the matter you've been working on until you hear from him."

"I see. You don't know what it's all about?"

"No, I most certainly . . . Dr. Jones called us this afternoon. She was most irate. She used words over the phone to Vernon that a woman simply should not use. I mean, really. Words *no* person should use."

"Do you know what it was about?"

"She said you had come out to the golf course to deliberately ruin her tournament chances. She wanted your . . . well, your body removed from anywhere near the Center forever. Really, Mr. Garrott, what did you do to that poor woman?"

"I believe I put a hook in her psyche."

"Well, whatever that is, you mustn't do it again. We can't afford to antagonize these people who have voting powers at the Center, Mr. Garrott. I thought she was going to have a heart seizure right there on the phone."

"That was unfortunate," Henry consoled, hoping his smile didn't project over the phone line. "I don't think it will happen again.

"By the way, Mrs. McCarthy, the other morning when I called and Vern was out running, did you have any difficulty finding him?"

"He was on the Crest Road where he usually runs."

"Fairly close to home?"

"No, he was about a mile down, toward the Center. Why do you ask? Say, are you thinking that Vernon . . . well, of all the nerve! Here we hire you to work for the Center when you're down on your luck, without even a job, and you have the nerve to suspect—"

"That's not quite the way it was."

"Talk about biting the hand that feeds you. After all we've done—" Click.

Henry was relieved at falling out of favor with Mrs. McCarthy. Being around fanatics had always made him uneasy, and Millie McCarthy, by virtue of her blind devotion to her husband, qualified her, in Henry's mind, as a fanatic. Perhaps not being in sympathy with McCarthy's over-all philosophy played a part in that judgment.

Henry mused for a moment, trying to construct a series of reasons and motives that could have placed Millie McCarthy on the scaffold with Dr. Robinson—but nothing came out right.

He dialed Miss Matthews' home.

"Hello, Mr. Garrott. How did you like the service this morning? I really didn't have an opportunity to chat with you afterwards."

"I especially liked the music."

"Yes, isn't our choir outstanding? And Dr. McDonally will be starting a mid-week study program on the minor prophets which will be of great interest."

"I'm afraid I won't be able to take advantage of that, Miss

Matthews. I don't think I'll be in town long enough.

"The reason I was calling ma'am, is this: Can you recall any instance at the Center when someone's mail was opened in error, and someone made a fuss about it—or perhaps an ex pected letter never arrived?"

"No, I can't remember any problem like that. There was an air-mail parcel sent to the wrong department which Dr. Jones made a fuss over, but we got that cleared up."

"Tell me about it."

"Oh, we had a senator's son helping in the mail room for a while, and he just put Dr. Jones' package in the wrong place. We finally found it in the storeroom the Life Sciences people use. He denied putting it there, of course, but like so many children of VIP's, he had a lazy streak."

"But Dr. Jones did finally get her package."

"Yes, and that was the end of it."

"She didn't complain about the contents being disturbed or anything of that sort?"

"No. I don't even know what was in the package. I'm sure she would have commented if anything was amiss. Dr. Jones is a real perfectionist. Say, how did you know about that? You certainly ask unusual questions." She laughed.

"When did this take place?"

"Well, it was shortly after Dr. Jones returned from Cleveland. I remember that, because she commented that a package would be arriving soon."

"And that was about when?"

"Oh, I'm so terrible about dates if I don't write them down. Their project fell through in February, I believe; then she took some time off. I imagine it was some time in March."

"Hmmm, well, thank you, Miss Matthews. I'll be coming by the Center in the morning to see Mr. McCarthy. I suppose I'll see you then."

"Oh, yes. I'm the first one there in the mornings, and usually the last one to leave at night. Old Reliable, you know." She laughed again and the yap of a small dog could be heard in the background. "Down, Toto. Be good now."

After hanging up, Henry conjured up an image of Miss Matthews sitting alone in her apartment with a small lap dog, and possibly a stand of African violets to keep her company. She had her church activities and possibly some other social contacts to keep her busy, although Henry doubted a woman who had moved about as much as she had would make friends easily at this point in her life. He wondered about her interests, what she had to look forward to, and if she were happy with her lot.

After showering, Henry opened the large folder Miss Matthews had given him that morning and started to sort through the public relations articles on the people from the Center.

Dr. Jones, after winning several amateur golf tournaments in the greater Cleveland area, joined the Ladies' Professional Golf Tour for two years before becoming a spokeswoman for a chain of sporting goods stores in Cleveland. She then co-founded the firm of Felcher-Jones Advertising, specializing in national surveys and test-market advertising.

It hardly seemed likely that she could have set up a business like that without at least picking up the basic rudiments of the financial structure. Nothing listed about a husband or family. Her hobbies, Henry noted with interest, included "an occasional round of golf for the fun of it" and collecting tomb relief rubbings from old European churches.

From Shoemaker's file he learned very little. Except for his years of Government service, when his position no doubt exposed him to budget-making and requisitions, he had no finance in his background. Ballard's and Begelman's profiles, while very complimentary and interesting, offered no help either.

As she promised, Miss Matthews had included a large folder on General Kilbourne, and as he thumbed through the many magazine articles she had copied, Henry noticed one four-page article from an old *Time* magazine cover story they had run on Kilbourne, near the end of the Second World War. It had been stapled together, while all the other articles were paper clipped. This struck Henry as rather unusual, especially since the staple was struck an inch or two into the body of the story. There were other stories on the first column of pages three and four, and it didn't affect his reading the article. But on the second page the staple came directly in the middle of a picture. After carefully removing the staple Henry saw it was a picture of Kilbourne in his old service uniform, complete with trench coat, disembarking a plane. At his side, with her arm affectionately laced through his, was a young W.A.C. with a smile from ear to ear. She was slender, her hair jet black, and a sparkle in the eyes that was now missing; but even so, it was not hard to recognize her as Marilyn Matthews, the last of the General's "Chief Administrators."

He called his family for the third time and finally got through. As he suspected, they had been out to dinner. Becky loved the new house and was dying to hear all about what her father was working on; she had seen Dr. Robinson's picture in the newspaper and was full of questions. Henry promised her a full report very shortly, but declined to get into it again on the phone.

Valery said they had been having a marvelous time. She decided she liked her children as adults even better than when they were little, and claimed if she were going to start another family, she would adopt them all at age sixteen.

Their cheerfulness only brought back Henry's lonesome blues, and he soon ran out of conversation. After hearing about some potentially serious problems with the upstairs plumbing, and that Valery had decided they needed to hire a gardener, he said good-bye.

Henry spent a restless night, with a recurring dream keeping his adrenalin running high. The young Miss Matthews, in her W.A.C. outfit, was somehow cast as Dorothy in the *Wizard of Oz*, and she was trying to water the African violets in her window box while a violent storm was raging outside. The first character to fly by her window was Dr. Jones with her number three wood. She was accusing Miss Matthews of taking her golf ball, and swung violently at the potted plants before the wind carried her out of sight.

Next came the Ballards in a row boat, with Tena at the oars. She was complaining about having to row, and Jeffry Ballard shouted back that he couldn't row because of the fish bowls he had to keep his hands in. Then he turned to Miss Matthews and started throwing goldfish at her by simply swinging the bowls about. It seemed it was her fault he had to keep the bowls on.

Next came a strawman, played half the time by Ray Bolger and half the time by Fyodor Begelman, who, with his bad leg, added a certain distinction to his part when it came his turn to dance.

The dream then became silly. People started changing roles at will. Part of the time it was Henry taking the abusive jibes, as Miss Matthews and he kept expecting McCarthy and his wife to ride by on a tandem bike, but they never showed. Neither did Wilma Robinson nor Jimmy Dill. Even near morning, when he could start willing certain acts to happen, he still couldn't see other people.

Monday

When Henry awoke, he'd perspired enough to warrant another shower. It would help clear his head, anyway. The confusing illusions of the night drifted away, and he found himself laughing at the events which a few minutes ago seemed so substantial.

But was there a shred of truth in the dream? People had suddenly turned hostile to him without what he considered valid reasons. McCarthy was mad because Henry was carrying the case too far; he would probably fire Henry, now that the big grant was coming through. Millie was upset because he insinuated her husband might be involved, which was understandable but not too rational.

Shoemaker was upset because he expected more from Henry—or was feigning being upset because he really was guilty. Dr. Jones was upset over her golf round . . . or because she wanted Henry out of the way. Begelman was upset because of a quirk in his stroke-affected brain or . . . Henry wondered if Begelman could climb a scaffold. He handled his dance assignment in the dream remarkably well. But what would be his purpose? What did he have to gain? Surely Dr. Robinson would not be his book's severest critic.

Henry found himself gyrating from highs to lows, psychologically, as he stood under the shower. The exhilaration of the chase had driven him beyond the restraints McCarthy had put on him—beyond reason and common sense, perhaps. Who was he to tackle such a project? If there were something to uncover, a team of policemen working slowly and meticulously would do a better job. So many interviews he'd botched up—alienating people, asking the wrong questions. Who did he think he was, Sherlock Holmes? Inspector Clouseau would be more efficient.

He shut off the water, dried himself, dressed, and dove eagerly into his devotions in the Psalms, for there was a balm in those pages that soothed his wounds. If the Lord would be steadfast with His servant David through his tribulations with King Saul, the Philistines, and finally, see him successfully through the attempted revolution, why wouldn't the Lord stand with him as well? The divine assurances, as well as the self-comparisons he made with the biblical hero, gave him a glow and momentum for the day.

O Lord, forget not thy servant Henry.

He arrived at the Center promptly at nine o'clock, as Mrs. McCarthy had asked him to do, but McCarthy was already occupied with someone else in his office. He sat and watched Miss Matthews flit in and out of the reception room, with her early morning secretarial tasks.

After emerging from Mr. McCarthy's office, she did a curious thing; she offered Henry some coffee, which he welcomed, but when she set down the tray, she placed it on the coffee table next to McCarthy's office, so Henry had to step across the room to help himself. When he did so, he noticed the door to McCarthy's office was ajar, and he could easily hear Vern McCarthy, in fine voice, responding to the questions of Officer Tugwell and someone else. Miss Matthews' downcast eyes gave Henry no indication the opportunity to eavesdrop had been intentional, but he was beginning to know her well enough to think it was.

"I told you all I know about the guy," McCarthy was saying. "He used to work for the CIA, but he had some kind of breakdown. Freaked out on a religious experience, I hear. Then he shows up here, probably trying to cash in on our former friendship in Europe and land a job with us or something."

"And you're sure he didn't know this Dr. Robinson before?" Tugwell asked.

"Of course he didn't. I just introduced him the day before."

"You don't think it a bit odd he should show up here early Saturday morning, just after Robinson falls to his death, then on Sunday he shows up just after a fire is discovered?" the third person in the room asked.

"The guy's a big pussy cat. A little weird but—"

"And then he goes around town talking to people he

doesn't know, who just *happen* to be working at the Center. Really, Mr. McCarthy."

"Who knows, maybe he was trying to milk them for a job, too."

"Doing what?"

"Search me. He's probably outside there now. Why don't you ask him?"

"But we're asking you. What is his connection with the Center?"

There was a long pause during which Henry could visualize McCarthy shrugging his shoulders. Tugwell continued.

"And you're sure he didn't know Shoemaker, either. Now Shoemaker used to work in Washington. What makes you think he didn't know him then?"

Henry put down his cup and stepped to the front of Miss Matthews' desk.

"What's the Amtrak schedule for today? Do you know?"

"Heading south?"

"Yes."

Without a hint of surprise, she thumbed her travel file for the schedule. Would you like to have me call the ticket counter?"

"I'll tell you in a few minutes," he advised. "You're a very fine secretary, Miss Matthews. It's been a joy watching you work."

"Thank you." She cooed with a smile rivaling Mona Lisa's.

Henry took another seat, away from the door, stared at the ceiling, and tried to think of King David. McCarthy must have let his guests out the side door, because when he burst into the reception room, there was no sign of them.

"Henry, old bean, how are you? Come in, come in," he gushed.

Henry went in and seated himself as far from the desk as he could.

"What are you sitting over there for?" McCarthy asked.

"You wanted to see me?"

McCarthy took the cue. He changed his mind about sitting behind his desk, and came over and sat near Henry. "Listen, I want to thank you for your help. I think we're going to call it quits on this investigation."

"I take it you got the grant."

"Yes. How 'bout that? The full grant. Everything we asked for," McCarthy declared with a broad smile.

"And you think it's wise to—"

"I think we've carried this about as far as necessary."

"I'd like to hear your reason for feeling that way," Henry said.

"It's obvious Shoemaker's our man. There's probably no chance in the world of recovering the money, so I think the best thing for all concerned is simply to drop it. I've got to think of what's best for the Center."

"And suppose it wasn't Shoemaker who embezzled."

"I've considered that, and I think just your presence here has served our purpose well. Anybody thinking of pulling more tricks will pull in their horns. We're hiring a bookkeeper, so the kind of circumstances we had before, with Begelman, won't occur again. I want to thank you for your help; I think your services have been well worth the five-thousand-dollar fee." He smiled benignly, as if expecting Henry to jump for joy at the mention of five thousand dollars.

"Vern, you're making a mistake. As an accountant, I've got to tell you this: Your first error was in not being on top of the finances when you first arrived. That error is understandable. You can justifiably plead ignorance of the initial problem, plus, you were no doubt in awe of Begelman and didn't want to challenge him—having just arrived and being dependent upon his good will. But now you're compounding the error by not following through—"

McCarthy was shaking his head. Henry shifted to his strongest argument.

"It'll just be a matter of time before we can trace those checks and find out who wrote—"

"No matter how you slice it, it all adds up to more bad publicity. Thanks, but no thanks.

"I know I promised you a check this morning. I was even prepared to trade in my wife's Mercedes in order to pay you, if you can believe that. But now, you're just going to have to wait. It won't be long."

"What's the matter, Vern? Afraid I'll show the check to Tugwell?"

McCarthy's face turned pale. Then his little eyes began blinking and darting about. "Something like that. Besides, I legally don't owe you a thing, the way you've been going beyond my instructions. But let's forget that. I want us to part friends. I'm sure you were doing what you thought was right."

McCarthy rose, sauntered over to his desk and started talking about the motel checkout time and the logistics of getting the Center's books back into McCarthy's hands. Both men were soon standing at the door, and McCarthy was extending his hand.

"Well, good-bye, Henry."

"Do me one last favor."

"What's that?"

"Have somebody check out Ballard's computer tapes."

"All right, if that's what it'll take to make you happy."

"Good-bye, Vern."

Miss Matthews was away from her desk. Perhaps she didn't like good-byes either. Henry strolled out into the Great Hall and took his last look around. Some of the maintenance people were tying off the loose ends of the model and taking various measurements and calculations, no doubt for its repair. The fellow who seemed to be in charge told the other men that Thursday was the deadline. Everything had to be in order for the press conference on that day.

Henry had a sense of missing out. Things would be happening, and he would not be included. It had been a very frustrating few days for him, and he should have been feeling good about getting out from under the whole mess, but the sense of incompleteness kept gnawing at him.

Back in his motel room, he went through the busy motions of a traveler. He secured the time of the morning train, called Valery and told her when to expect him, then called the police station as Tugwell asked him to, leaving his home address and phone number. He stuffed the Center's books back into the small briefcase and called the town's only messenger service, as McCarthy had instructed.

By the time he reached the train station, he was tired, but he had managed to put some emotional distance between himself and the Kilbourne Center problems.

"Expecting rain, are you?" a familiar voice jeered from behind him. Henry turned to see Tugwell climbing out of his squad car.

"Oh, hello. The umbrella is the wife's idea. I called your station."

"Yeah, I know. I got the message." He walked at Henry's side toward the ticket counter. "You got a little time before the train pulls out? I'll buy you a cup of coffee."

"All right."

Henry purchased his ticket, and the two men settled in a scarred little booth in the station's small snack shop. Tugwell hadn't spoken his mind, and Henry decided to sip his coffee and concentrate on devouring his sweetroll until he did.

"This seems to be my day for seeing people off."

"Oh?" Henry grunted between sips.

"I really came by to thank you for the tip. That was a stroke of genius."

"What tip was that?"

Tugwell smiled and poured cream in his coffee until it turned pale. "You really don't have to play cat and mouse with me, you know. We know who you are, and we have a pretty good idea what you're doing here, in spite of McCarthy's little games. This is a small town, you know."

"I'm relieved to hear that." In response to Tugwell's sarcastic glance he added, "Really I am. But I still don't know what tip you're talking about."

Tugwell leaned his elbow against the counter and the dingy wall. "Yesterday when you asked Shoemaker about Robinson's homosexual ties, Shoemaker got mad, remember?"

"I don't know if 'mad' is the right term. Disgusted might be—"

"The deputy told me 'mad.' Anyway, it got me thinking about the whole thing. You and I've been barking up the wrong tree. We figured it was all about something sophisticated and complicated, because we're dealing with a bunch of brains. But that wasn't it at all. They're people with emotions, just like the rest of us.

"I'd been trying to come up with a motive that would fit this Shoemaker character, and all I could see was what everyone else saw. His theory about the inferiority of black-skinned people made Robinson his natural enemy. But that only gave motivation for Robinson to kill *him*—not the other way around. Killing a black, even by accident, could only hurt Shoemaker. But then when you said that bit about queers, it all came together.

"The NAACP, and plenty of other groups, have been trying to shut Shoemaker up. They've picketed his speeches and thrown rocks at his car. Back in Detroit last year, a gang even wrecked a TV studio where he was trying to debate. They'd go to just about any length to shut him up.

"Then comes their golden opportunity. Dr. Robinson gets invited to join the staff, or maybe he was planted. It struck me as being a bit unusual to have Robinson here. Several told me he wasn't a research scientist—just your run-of-the-mill M.D., but here he gets on the staff."

"You mean, you think he had an ulterior motive?"

"Of course. Look at the facts. He sets up his experiments like somebody told him to, then he forgets about them— because he's really here to get the goods on Shoemaker to blackmail him, if you will, into keeping quiet."

"And what kind of goods is he supposed to have on Shoemaker?"

Tugwell smiled, "You've already told me. The way I see it is this: The blacks checked into Shoemaker's background and found some evidence that indicated Shoemaker had homosexual tendencies—but not strong enough evidence to blackmail him. So they send this Robinson out here, and Robinson, who may be a bit of a swish himself, ingratiates himself with our little clutch of queers in the art community and finds out Shoemaker is up to his old tricks again. He confronts Shoemaker with the new evidence, but Shoemaker turns the tables on him and kills him to keep him silent."

"I can't buy that," Henry said.

"Why not?"

"Well, number one, there's no evidence to suggest that

Shoemaker is a que . . . is homosexual—"

"Ah but there is. After your comment yesterday, I put the question to our M.O. computer in Omaha, and what do you think pops out? Shoemaker was arrested in '61 when he was student teaching in a little college back east. He had something going with one of the male students; they got caught, and he was discharged."

"Maybe it was an isolated incident."

Tugwell shook his head. "People have a boring habit of repeating themselves."

"I could argue the point, but let's assume you're right. I don't think the threat of such an exposure would be enough to drive a 'sophisticated man' like Shoemaker to commit murder. Not in this day and age."

"Oh, you bet it would. He comes from a very straight-laced old family in Philadelphia. His father was an Episcopalian High Church Priest."

"You're kidding."

"And an uncle was on the State Supreme Court."

"That surprises me. Then why didn't he get family connections out here to help him . . . ?" Henry didn't finish because the answer had dawned on him.

"Yeah, you know why. Because he didn't want his family to get involved. He even gave us his wrong middle name to throw us off the track."

Henry was scowling out the window, absently watching a mother with two children waiting for the train. He was trying to find holes in Tugwell's theory, perhaps because he didn't want to see the thing end like this.

"What did Ballard have to say when you talked to him?"

Tugwell laughed. "I wondered how long it would take you to get around to him. He's the one that really clinched this thing for me. I had to badger it out of the guy, but he finally admitted Robinson told him that he, Robinson, was going to have it out with Shoemaker over a personal problem."

"Did he say when Robinson planned to 'have it out'?"

Tugwell squirmed. "Well, no, but he implied it would be soon."

"And did he say anything about homosexuality?"

"No. Just that it was a personal matter. I hardly think Robinson would go blabbing the subject around if he intended to use the information for blackmail purposes."

"That's not exactly an iron-clad case you've got there."

"It'll hold up okay for murder-two. I kinda think it was a spur-of-the-moment thing anyway. Maybe even an accident in a shoving match. There's an awfully good chance of a person surviving a fall of thirty-seven-and-a-half feet. Not exactly a sure-fire method of killing somebody."

"If it wasn't premeditated, then how do you explain the fire?"

"Probably something he thought of later." Tugwell shrugged. "He had plenty of time to do that between the time we questioned him and when we arrested him. We figure he was destroying blackmail evidence Robinson had on the premises."

"But why start a fire? Why not just take the evidence?"

"Because he didn't have time. He may have heard our men in the other part of the building anyway."

Henry could see so many other holes in Tugwell's theory, but he decided not to verbalize them. Why would Shoemaker mess around with the candle and the special fuse? Such work would take pre-planning and time enough at the location to get the paper set right, etc. And still, no mention of the missing funds. If Tugwell did in fact know why Henry had come to town, he apparently made no connection between the two events.

The sound of a train was heard in the distance, and Tugwell reached for the check.

"Who else have you been seeing off?" Henry asked.

"What? Oh, Ballard, poor guy. His wife had to be hospitalized last night with premature labor pains. He can't take care of himself very well with his hands immobilized, so he went up to Carmel where his parents live. I put him on the plane this morning."

Henry had seen this pattern so often before; the innocent bystanders are inevitably the ones who get hurt the most. As the two men ambled toward the train, Henry recalled the way Tena Ballard had taken the incorrigible little McCarthy boy into her arms, and the way she had struggled to hold back her tears when Ballard reached over to give her hand a squeeze.

"Oh, I almost forgot," Tugwell said, reaching into his breast pocket. He pulled out an envelope which he handed to Henry. "Your subpeona. We wouldn't want you to think we don't want you back in our fair community. A little reading material for the ride—you've got a long way to go."

"So have you, I'm afraid. Thanks for the coffee."

Henry started to board, but Tugwell grabbed his arm. "What do you mean? Come on now, level with me."

"All I know is there are too many questions going begging. Shoemaker may be your man, but there are still too many loose ends to close the case. Why did Robinson send for a postal inspector?"

"What has that got to do—?"

"Why was water sprayed in the attic area so the roofer wouldn't have to be paid?"

"What's that?"

Henry stepped on board. It felt good to vent his feelings. He rattled more questions at Tugwell who took it all in, open-mouthed. Henry concluded, "And you might ask McCarthy why I'm leaving without finishing the job I came to do."

The last statement was shouted out as the train rolled away. Tugwell stood on the platform with his hands on his hips, then turned and slowly walked toward his car.

Henry had not wanted to violate McCarthy's secrets, but the frustration he felt made him feel justified in slipping Tugwell a few hints. If he couldn't be on hand himself to see this thing through, he at least wanted to leave Tugwell with some of his own doubts. Especially now, when Henry had a pretty good idea how the lab coat got into Shoemaker's file drawer.

The girls were at the station to welcome the weary traveler home. "Girls" was the right term, for Valery was acting more youthful and giggly than Henry had seen her in years. It was good to hear her laughing again. Henry embraced them both warmly, and especially enjoyed the look he and Becky exchanged after their hug. There was love in her face, but more than that, Henry saw an understanding and anticipation that excited him.

If any of their three children had been problem children, it was Becky. She had been very headstrong as a child, and had been the cause of more breakdowns in family discipline than the older two combined. Henry, on occasion, had accused Valery of being too strict with the older ones and too lenient with "the baby." But Valery had insisted she acted the same with them all, but her energy level was falling short with little Miss Activity.

After much pleading and whining on her part, Becky had been permitted to spend her last two years of high school in the States. Then, three years of college, with only brief holiday trips home, made her something of a stranger to her parents. Now, getting reacquainted with the adult version was turning out to be a pleasant surprise.

On the way home, Becky leaned forward from the back seat of the Volvo, just the same way she had done as a little girl, and chatted about the strange sights in Southern California.

"Think you're going to like it here?" Henry asked.

"Sure. But I still plan to finish school back east."

"Say, what happened to your summer plans to tour Europe? Your mother says you were canceled out."

"Right. Something about the exchange rate. I guess they don't like American money anymore."

"You sorry?"

"Not really. I figure if the Lord wants me to see Europe, I'll see Europe. He just has something else in mind for me, that's all."

"Hmm," Henry responded, and drove on without further comment.

"Daddy, don't you think all things work out for the best for those who love the Lord?"

"I don't know. I haven't thought much about it. I do think your attitude toward disappointments is an improvement over your earlier one. Remember the crying jag you went on when I had to cancel out on taking you to that ice skating party in Amsterdam?"

Becky laughed. "I was a real pain, wasn't I?"

"Let's just say you kept us very active," Valery corrected.

"I'm sorry," Becky said, and touched the side of her mother's cheek.

They rode in silence while Henry performed the necessary lane changing and jostling to get them away from the airport.

Once on the freeway, Becky began, "You know what I was thinking? Maybe the Lord wants me to help you with this mysterious business up at the Kilbourne Center."

Henry and Valery exchanged patronizing smiles.

"No, I'm serious. My professors say I have a very analytical mind. I'd make a great detective. Really, I would."

"Maybe you would, honey, but I've been taken off the job. I was actually invited up to look into a financial problem, but it seemed to be tied in with this death of Dr. Robinson."

"Did you really find him the way the paper described?"

"Yes, I did."

"Tell us about it."

Henry glanced at Valery. "You sure you want to hear all this?"

"Oh yes, Mother, you do. And don't leave out any of the gory details," Becky chirped, bouncing with excitement.

"First of all, tell us about your wrist. How is it?" Valery asked.

"It seems to be fine. Just a stupid accident," Henry muttered, and proceeded to recount the events, including his fall at the Center, how Dr. Robinson had correctly diagnosed the problem, and then, the early morning appointment Henry had arranged with the doctor.

"As a matter of fact, Becky, when I arrived at the Center, I stood by my car for a moment to enjoy the beautiful sunrise. Perhaps if I hadn't done that but gone straight to the door and knocked just a few minutes earlier, Dr. Robinson might be alive today. How does *that* tie in with your theory about all things working together for good?"

"Welll," Becky drawled, and scratched her chin. "I think there are always going to be evil and bad things happening in life . . . until the Lord comes. But even the bad things can't separate us from the goodness of God."

Valery turned and looked straight into the face of her offspring. "Where on earth? Where do you come up with such thoughts? Isn't all this rather simplistic?"

Becky laughed, "Oh, Mother," and reached over to give her a tight hug, which disturbed both Valery's coiffure and composure.

"Becky, there are people in other cars—heavens. Where did you learn to be so demonstrative?"

"We never hugged enough when I was growing up. I'm just making up for lost time," Becky teased. "I figure one good hug is worth three philosophical arguments any day."

Henry laughed. "How about that, Val?" he said, and tried to put his arm around his wife, but she resisted.

"Watch where you're going! Honestly. I'm suddenly in a family of religious weirdos. Go back to your conversation about the Kilbourne Center."

This they did, after a little more kidding at Valery's expense. Becky frequently interrupted to clarify points Henry had jumped over too quickly, demonstrating a very quick grasp of the situation. With such an attentive listener, Henry related the events of his long weekend with more enthusiasm than he knew he had left in him. All the way home, the events flowed, Henry gesticulating and explaining, and Becky near his shoulder spurring him on with her youthful expressions and questions.

Once they reached their new home, the storytelling was briefly side-tracked with preparations for the evening meal.

The house was filled with the inviting aroma of roast leg of lamb. Henry had never expressed a preference for lamb, but invariably, Valery, on special occasions when she wanted to prepare something extra nice, had resorted to lamb. The table was set on the patio, and Valery, for the first time, made practical use of her mother's large ancient serving cart by bringing out all the food in one trip.

It was a leisurely, chatty dinner, with the conversation, no matter what tangent it started out on, invariably returning to the matter up the coast. As they talked, the setting sun played its tricks on the colorful flowers in the garden. First, the orange flower petals turned pale, then the reds, then for a short time the blues; finally, the blues and greens lost their definition, and darkness fell.

Valery had cleared the table and washed the dishes, while Henry and Becky, now in a quieter mood, still pursued their favorite topic.

"Say, you two," Valery called, coming out of the house with two sweaters in hand, "it's getting chilly out here. Once the sun goes down here on the coast, it turns cool. Not like back east."

"You know, you're right," Henry agreed. He rubbed his arms and dutifully put on his sweater.

"But what about this Ballard?" Becky probed. "Why would his name appear intermittently on the bad checks, while the other names were all lumped together? Was he gone like the others during those times?"

"I don't know. Miss Matthews confirmed the other people were away from the Center when their bogus checks were cleared, but I didn't get around to finding out about Ballard. You think he's our culprit?"

"Nno. My money's still on McCarthy."

"Why?"

"I just can't see a person not wanting to know what happened to that $700,000. That's an awful lot of cash."

"You have to remember his background," Henry reminded. "He's used to working with large sums in the State Department, and I think he'd feel that would be a small price to pay to hold together the good name of the Center."

"But he could have had you find out quietly."

Henry laughed. "I wasn't a very good boy in that regard. And every time I turned up, I was accompanied by the police or the fire departments. I think the clanging of bells behind me finally got to him.

"What do you think of Dr. Jones? She had the most to gain."

Becky rubbed her chin with her thumb. "Yeess, but I don't really know enough about her. Does a professional woman kill for revenge?"

"Oh, I'm sure it's happened."

"And how would the money tie in?"

"Perhaps she simply wanted it for herself," Henry suggested. "Now that her big project has fallen through . . . I don't know what her plans are."

"Is she working on anything else for the Center?"

"I don't know. I didn't get a chance to find out. But, we do know her sponsor, Bertha Corbut, is dead, so I would guess her future with the Center is rather bleak."

They sat thinking for a moment, then Becky caught herself in the midst of an involuntary yawn. "Oh, excuse me." She laughed.

"Say, do you realize what time it is by Becky's system clock?" Valery asked her husband. "She's going to be a jet lag casualty if we don't get her into bed."

"I know, Mother, but I just hate to go to bed until we get this settled."

They both laughed at their daughter and made the usual parental comments about the impatience and the impertinence of youth. But at the same time, the preparations for the night were made, and within half an hour the house was still. It felt good in Henry's bones to be home with his loved ones.

At four-fifteen in the morning, Henry looked at the clock, quietly put on his robe and slippers, and headed toward the kitchen. After some rummaging about, he found where Valery had hidden his favorite saucepan, and proceeded to heat himself some milk. He stood at the sink window, staring out at nothing in particular, and rubbing his stomach, when his first guest arrived.

"Daddy?"

"Hi. What are you doing up?"

"This is the time I usually get up back east. What are you doing up?"

"Oh, I had another dream. I thought maybe some milk would settle me down."

"You look flushed," Becky said checking his forehead. "What did you dream about?"

"You don't want to hear about it. We might wake your mother."

"No, no, I do," she insisted, sliding onto a bar stool. "Dreams can be very important. I took a class on dreams and their meaning; my teacher said your subconscious is frequently trying to tell you something. It's just a matter of figuring out your individual code your dreams come in."

"What's this about dreams?" Valery asked, wrapping her robe about herself. "Don't you people know what time it is?"

"Daddy's had another dream."

"Henry, not again. You and your dreams."

"Sit down, Mom. He's going to tell us about it."

Valery turned down the flame under the milk and joined her daughter. "I don't know what all this is supposed to prove. I have a wallpaper man coming at nine in the morning."

"Now, be quiet and listen," Becky ordered, taking Valery's hand.

"It seemed to be about Dr. Robinson," Henry began. "Now that I think about it, I don't know why I was so excited. But during the dream I was very distraught, or upset, about something. It seems I was on a busy, very crowded street somewhere. I was up above, looking down, sort of like those old newsreel camera shots of teeming American city dwellers. Anyway, the people all came to a corner and waited at a curb for the streetlights to change. While they were standing there, I could see Dr. Robinson and several other blacks in the crowd. All the others seemed to be young boys in dirty, torn, old T-shirts and scruffy clothes; they were waiting with everyone else for the light to change. The lights were unusual too. They were the usual green-yellow-red variety but there was a clock face on each of the lights.

"Finally the light changed to green and people all started across. All, that is, except Dr. Robinson and the black boys. It was as though they were waiting for the light to do a special thing, just for blacks. So, instead of crossing the street with the others, they paraded back and forth along the curb, chanting like protesters, 'The time is out of joint, the time is out of joint.'"

"And then what?" Becky asked.

"Nothing. That's all there was. I woke up very disturbed. But now, for the life of me, I can't think of what I was disturbed about.

"There's enough milk here for two of us. Either of you want some?"

"You know it doesn't agree with me," Valery said.

"I'll have some," Becky said, fetching the mugs. "Let's see if we can figure this out. The obvious thing is the quote from Shakespeare. Hamlet said about the untimely death of his father, 'The time is out of joint, oh cursed spite that ever I was born to set it right.' That would mean you, Daddy. Since it was your dream, I'd say you have to make something right."

"Yes, but what? I thought that's what I'd been trying to do."

"And the clocks on the lights and the other reference to time . . . let's see . . . you were very disturbed, too. Maybe something needs to be done soon, or right away."

"Yes," Henry said. "Robinson had said, 'Time is of the essence.' And he seemed very disturbed too, the day before his death—and the look in his eyes when he fell. I thought it was just because of the fall and his injury, but now I'm not so sure."

They all sat gazing at one another. Then Becky remarked, "Why didn't they want to cross the street with the others? Why would they refuse? Any ideas, Mother?"

"I have an idea. Maybe roast lamb no longer agrees with your father."

"Oh, Mother!"

"He's always had strange dreams. They don't mean anything. I think it's just nature's way of letting us recharge our batteries. You start putting credence to what happens in dreams and there's no telling how far afield you'll go. Look, the horizon's starting to light up. Let's get to bed now and try to get some sleep."

They all shuffled off to their beds again after a few sips of milk, shaking their sleepy heads.

Henry was sure he had been asleep again for only a second when someone started jostling him about.

"Daddy, Daddy, wake up!"

"Huh, who, what is it?"

"Daddy, I've figured it out."

"Becky. This is getting ridiculous. We've got to get some sleep, honey."

"Come on, Daddy. You can sleep on the plane."

"Plane? What plane?" Henry blinked helplessly.

"Becky, are you out of your mind?" her mother mumbled. "It's five o'clock."

Becky bounced on the bed and two heads bobbed. "Listen! I've figured it out! Or rather, you did in your dream, Daddy. Only we had one thing wrong. The blacks didn't refuse to cross the street. They didn't cross the street because they couldn't cross the street."

She ran the extension phone over to Henry's side of the bed. "Hurry, Daddy. Call the airport and find out what's the earliest flight to Cleveland."

Tuesday

"May I help you?" the attractive young receptionist asked.

"Yes. This is the Felcher National Agency, isn't it?" Henry asked.

"That's what it says on the door. Oh, is the young lady talent? They won't be reading for the part until tomorrow, but you can leave her pictures."

"No, no. I think you misunderstand. We're not here about a commercial. We'd like to see whoever's in charge of your national testing service."

"Mr. Bowling is out of the country, and his assistant, Ms. Philips, I believe, has left for the day."

"Would you check please? It's vitally important," Henry said.

"I see," the young lady said, looking first at Henry, then Becky, and back again. They must have proved a bit of an oddity to the young receptionist. Both of them were carrying suitcases still bearing airport tags, and were slightly out of breath.

"Your name please, and what is your business?" she asked, reaching for the phone.

"Garrott. She won't know me. Tell her it's an important matter about the Kilbourne Center."

Ms. Philips was in after all, and she could spare a few minutes. The travelers found a corner for their suitcases, and hurried through the massive double doors of the agency, past the secretarial pool, and finally into Ms. Philips' office—or rather a planning room she seemed to be using as an office. There were large charts and graphs on easels, as well as charts on the walls. A battery of television screens were built into the paneled wall opposite a small conference table. Ms. Philips was a tall, slender woman, dressed in a tailored business suit.

"Please come in and sit down over here, by me, Mr. Garrott and Miss . . . "

"I'm Becky Garrott, his daughter."

"Very pleased to meet you both."

The three of them sat at one end of the conference table where Ms. Philips seemed to be making her desk.

"Oh, Betty," she called to the retreating receptionist who had just shown them in. "Would you have my secretary bring in the files on the Kilbourne account? They're in the inactive cabinet, I think.

"Now, Mr. Garrott, what can we do for you? I do have an early dinner appointment south of town, so this will have to be brief, I'm sorry to say. It would have been better if you had called."

"Ms. Philips, we did not call for a specific reason. We're here to check on a shipment of a sample product your agency has been directed to make."

"By whom?" Ms. Philips asked.

"By someone at the Kilbourne Center."

"Kilbourne? Are you sure you have the right agency?"

"Didn't Bertha Corbut and Dr. Jones have a government-related project with this agency?"

"Yes, indeed. The regional branch of our company still

bears Dr. Jones' name, and I know of her project very well—I was account executive. But that account has been dormant since last February."

"Are you certain of that? I mean, isn't there a possibility that part of their project could be continuing under a different name?"

Another attractive young secretary came in with two file folders which she deposited in front of Ms. Philips.

"Thank you," Ms. Philips said, and flipped open the larger folder. She removed a ledger and opened it to the page of the last entry. "See here? The last bill for agency services was mailed February 22 and paid March 23."

Henry turned his head to better read the entries and flipped back a page. "Is there a possibility some assignment had been prepaid and the work not completed until recently?"

"We don't bill in that manner, Mr. Garrott," she replied, turning the ledger so it was more difficult for Henry to read. "Perhaps if you could explain to me the nature of your problem."

With his eyes fixed on the book, Henry said, "We are afraid something is going to be distributed to a segment of the public that . . . should not be distributed. Addresses may have been stolen which are about to be used on your addressing machines."

"I see . . . what is your position with the Kilbourne people?"

"I've just completed a job with them, but I'm not now. . . . Ms. Philips, this could possibly be a very important matter. Are there any other firms on the west coast which you have started doing testing for within the past year or six months?"

She closed the folder. "Mr. Garrott, I'm sure you can understand we can't disclose such information. Sample market testing of new products suffers from a very high incidence of industrial espionage. We have to do everything we can to keep the lid on our clients' information. Now, you really will have to excuse me." She rose and reached for her jacket.

"Yes, of course. Thanks for seeing us. Come on, Becky."

Henry hurried out into the secretarial pool with Becky following. He went to one of the empty desks and jotted something on a note pad.

"She wasn't very helpful, was she?" Becky said. "What do we do now? What's that you're writing?"

"The name of their products distribution center. See that phone book there? Look up the address of Henning Distributors and Imports."

"Okay," Becky said, "but you've lost me. Where did you get that name?"

"It was on the next-to-last page of the entries."

"How could you possibly pick that out?"

"I can read upside down. A little trick the CIA thought might be helpful. You find it yet?"

"Here it is."

While Becky was writing down the address, Ms. Philips came out of her office loaded down with a large purse and an oversized briefcase. She gave the Garrotts a cool look, then hurried out through the double doors.

"She's a cold fish, isn't she? You think she knows more than she's telling?" Becky asked.

"For the moment we'll have to assume she doesn't," Henry stated, then asked a nearby secretary, "May I use this phone for a local call?"

"Why don't you use the one in there? There'll be less noise."

Henry thanked her, and he and Becky stepped into a small adjoining office. He dialed the number, then asked to speak to the dispatcher. When that terminology didn't work, he asked to talk to the dock foreman. While waiting for the foreman, Henry covered the mouthpiece and questioned Becky. "Well, what do you think? You still feel the stuff would be in toothpaste?"

"Yes, I'm certain. It's the only thing it could be in."

"Okay, we'll give it a shot," Henry whispered. "Hello, yes, this is Henry Garrott. I'm calling from Felcher Advertising Agency, and I was wondering if the rush order of toothpaste samples had come in yet?"

"Say, you people better get your wires straight," the gruff voice bellowed. "Are they 'sposed to mail 'em, or are we?"

"What do you mean?"

"I mean, just before noon we got a call from the Effervescent Smile people that they was going to do the mailing, and we sent all the labels over there."

"How come the switch?" Henry asked authoritatively.

"Listen, my people here already got all the overtime they want. I couldn't guarantee any midnight mailing deadline. Ms. Philips said it was okay to send the labels. Don't you people talk to each other?"

"Yes, it's okay. But what plant are they shipping from?"

"What plant? The only plant they got, man."

"But can you give me the address? I'm new at this."

"It used to be the old Proctor and Gamble plant next to the brewery. It's Riverfront and Sixth, I think—Sixth or Seventh."

"Thank you; you've been most helpful," Henry said. "By the way, you sent all the labels? How many individual packages did that make again?"

"Six hundred and twenty-five thousand."

Henry hung up. His face was ashen.

"Six hundred and twenty-five thousand. Now we know what happened to the Kilbourne seven hundred thousand."

"That's an awful lot of samples, and if they're mailed to the right people . . . Do you think we'd better call the police?"

"He mentioned a midnight shipping deadline. Let's see if we can get ahold of one of those samples first. You say it won't be hard to detect?" he asked as they started for the door.

"All we need to do is get a smear under a microscope. The little buggers should be wiggling all over the place."

"Good. It'll be a lot easier to get police cooperation if we have one to show. Stopping the U.S. mail is not a simple matter."

"Then let's try to get it stopped before they deliver any to the post office," Becky suggested, picking up her suitcase.

"Do you have any idea how many six hundred and twenty-five thousand is?" Henry asked. "Even in small packages, that's a lot of toothpaste. They're probably sending it over to the post office as fast as it comes off their assembly line."

They hailed a cab and dropped their suitcases at a small motel en route. Back in the cab, Henry reviewed the events that had brought them this far—how people return to the areas that are familiar to them, how the study of a criminal's mode of operation so frequently leads to his capture, and that it wasn't so unusual to find the person they were pursuing using the services of people previously contacted.

It was mostly nervous talk, because they both realized the enormity of their task. When he noticed Becky was nodding in agreement with his comments more out of courtesy than from genuine interest, Henry silenced himself. After several blocks Becky's hand reached over and grabbed his. It was a firm, tense grip. She prayed, "O Lord, we just pray that you'll be with us in a special way the next few hours. Help us to do what you want done. And keep us safe. Amen."

"Amen," Henry intoned.

"There it is," Henry said, looking out at a three-story brick building occupying a large corner lot in an older, industrial section of town. A large yellow sign, covering part of the third story, proclaimed: "Give your teeth to Effervescent Smile"; a large set of lips and teeth smiled down on the passersby.

The cabbie pulled up at the delivery gate and Henry asked him to wait. He'd wait all right, but he'd have to be paid for the first ride. Henry was already tense, and the cabbie's gruff manner only irritated him more. He tossed the money in the window and muttered, "You'll owe me fifty-five cents."

They stepped briskly through the unattended gate toward the large loading dock. There were two single-axle trucks waiting for loads, and the noise from the interior of the building convinced Henry things were humming. Becky was trailing him by a stride, and Henry turned around to see her looking about apprehensively.

"Come on, honey, let's see some confidence—like we belong here."

They took a few more steps before they were stopped by a uniformed guard coming out of the building with a coffee cup in his hand. "Can I help you folks?"

"Yes. We're here to pick up one of the toothpaste samples for testing," Henry said.

"I don't have any paper work on that. What's the name, please?"

"You wouldn't have it yet. We just came from the agency, and we talked to the dock foreman over at Henning Distributors. Garrott's the name."

"Hold on, now," the guard insisted, and flipped through several small pieces of paper he had attached to an old clipboard near the dock. "You can't go in if you're not on the list. You'll have to go 'round to the receptionist's desk."

"Look, this is the pick-up dock, isn't it?" Henry asked, while walking and pushing Becky along ahead of him. "We're here to pick up one little tiny sample for testing."

"But I ain't got you on my list."

Just then another truck pulled up to the gate. The driver impatiently honked and yelled out for the guard. The poor gentleman spilled part of his coffee trying to go in three directions at once—chasing after Henry, checking his clipboard, and responding to the newly arrived trucker. Finally he called out to someone on the dock, "Murray, will you see what these people want?" and trotted back to the truck at the gate.

"What can I do for you folks?" Murray asked, taking off his gloves and leaning against some of the boxes waiting to be loaded.

"Is this part of the rush toothpaste order?" Henry said, coming up the dock steps.

"Yeah, all this is. It's our only job right now."

Henry spotted a large box-opener with a razor blade protruding from one end. "Mind if I borrow this?"

"Hey! What're you doing?"

"We need one of the tubes for testing," Henry demanded, readying the blade to slice into one of the sealed cardboard boxes.

Murray grabbed for the box. "Hey, wait a minute. Are you with the Peabody people?"

"From the west coast."

"Look, I'll get you one from a box that ain't been sealed up yet. The post office don't like it when we send zip coded boxes that ain't sealed."

"Fine."

"You just need one tube?" he called, starting down a corridor with Henry and Becky close behind.

"That's all."

"How come you didn't come by when we were mixing this morning. That woulda been the time to do your testing."

"We were on an airplane this morning."

"I thought Mr. Peabody did all the testing when he put in the color dye this morning."

"This is another type of test we need to do. Mr. Peabody added the dye himself, you say?"

"Yeah, he was awful particular about it. He said the colors had to be just right to appeal to the kids."

Henry and Becky exchanged knowing glances. Then Henry asked, "Is it usual to ship samples the same day they're made up, like this?"

"I can't recall our ever doing it like this before."

They came into a large assembly room, where several rows of women were packaging small sample boxes into larger boxes. Murray reached over and grabbed one of the samples. "Here you go."

Henry found the box was already addressed to someone in Oakland, California, and there was first-class postage on it. The box itself was designed like a child's racing car, with snap-out wheels and an aerodynamic design on one end of the box to simulate a rakish front end and windshield. Inside was a small tube with the Effervescent Smile label designed to appeal to children.

"Thanks, this will do just fine," Henry said. "By the way, is Mr. Peabody still here?"

"Sure, I'll show you." He led them to the center of the room where the work area was two stories high. "Right up there." He pointed to a catwalk.

Henry hung back behind some tall machinery so that anyone on the catwalk could not see him. "Where?" he asked.

"Right up there. The dude in the white gloves."

Henry peeked around the corner and saw Jeffry Ballard leaning on the guard rail watching the work progressing in another area of the plant floor. He was in a business suit and wore a pair of white gloves over his injured hands.

"It's Ballard all right," he said to Becky, and the two of them started edging out the same way they came in.

"You want me to let him know you're here for the sample?" Murray asked.

"No, that won't be necessary. You've been very helpful, Murray."

"Hey now, what's going on? You do work for him, don't you?"

"You'll read all about it in the papers. Thanks again."

Becky and Henry exited carefully. There was one open space of ten feet they would have to cross before they reached the door to the corridor where Ballard could no longer see them. As they crossed the area Henry held up a piece of cardboard over his face to shield his identity from Ballard. Ballard didn't see him, but Murray did. He stood scowling at them, slapping his work gloves into his bare hand.

The Garrotts raced down the corridor, then slowed to a hurried walk along the dock, down the dock steps, and across the yard to the gate. The guard was there, finishing his coffee. He looked up and scowled as they went past.

"Got what we came for," Henry called. "Thanks again."

Outside the gate, they both dashed to the cab.

"Okay, let's go. Quick!" Henry barked to the driver, who was leaning against the front fender smoking and watching the traffic up the street. He looked around and grimaced at the two in the back seat.

"Hurry, man! We gotta go!"

"Just finishing up my smoke. You mind?"

"Please, we're in a very big hurry," Becky called. "Finish it in the cab. We don't mind at all."

The cabbie took one more long deliberate drag on his cigarette, snapped it away, and ambled into his place behind the wheel. "I'm not exactly wild, you know, about having money thrown at me, mister."

"What?"

"My fare. You threw the money right in my face like I was a dog, or somethin'. That's no way to treat a person, you know."

All of this lecture was made before the engine was started. The cabbie was fussing with a knob on his two-way radio, and Henry and Becky were dividing their attention between him and the gate behind them.

"You're right. I apologize," Henry said. "That was a very

inconsiderate way for me to act. But we are in a very great hurry. Won't you please—"

"Okay, okay." He finally started the cab, but before moving, he contacted his dispatch operator on the radio to give his location and destination. "Where to, mister?"

"Just drive, okay?"

But before he could throw it in gear, they heard the slapping of running feet behind them and Ballard's voice shouting.

"Wait! Stop! Wait a minute!"

He slammed up against the cab, then peered into the back seat. He was breathing heavily but didn't say anything for a moment, just staring wildly at Henry and Becky through the open window. He gasped, "Where're you going? What are you going to do?"

"What do you think?" Henry muttered. "Let's go, driver."

The engine revved.

"No, no, wait. I've got to talk to you," Ballard pleaded. He tried to open the car door with the heels of his gloved hands but didn't have the strength to do it.

"I don't think we have anything to talk about."

"Yes, we do! It isn't what you think. You've got to listen to me."

His face was pale and taut, and there were blotches of blood seeping through his gloves; it was not difficult to feel sorry for the man. Henry looked at Becky. She shook her head.

"Please. I'm not going to do anything to you. What could I do? I can't even open this door."

"Look, mister," the cabbie snarled, "is it in or out? Let's get the show on the road."

Now he was in a hurry.

Henry reached over and opened the door for Ballard. He got in and kicked down one of the jump seats in front of Becky and Henry. "Thanks."

"Where to?" the cabbie repeated, irritably.

"Downtown, police headquarters," Henry ordered, watching Ballard's eyes.

"Are you sure you know what you're doing?" Ballard begged.

"We'll soon know when we get this analyzed."

Ballard's eyes followed the toothpaste sample as Henry moved it from one hand to the other and dropped it in the side pocket of his coat.

Ballard laughed nervously. "What is it you think you've discovered?"

"I think you've taken it upon yourself to sterilize a large portion of the black population of the United States."

"What?" He laughed again, but reached up and swung closed the glass partition between the driver and passengers. "How did you come to such an outlandish conclusion?"

"This is my daughter, Becky Garrott. Professor Ballard."

They exchanged nods as the cab pulled out into traffic.

"Becky finally figured out what was happening," Henry revealed. "Her science background turned the whole puzzle around. You see, I mentioned to her that Dr. Robinson had a refrigerator full of antibiotic medicines. He had mentioned this to me when I needed some help with my hand. Now, that didn't mean anything to me, but Becky knew most such medicines have a relatively short shelf-life, and are quite expensive. Please correct me if I'm wrong."

"No, please go on. I'm fascinated," Ballard mocked.

"So why, we wondered, would a doctor who was out of medical practice be stocking such drugs in his home? Who would he be treating but himself or someone close by; someone he would be seeing in the normal course of his day? Then I remembered he was keeping himself physically apart from his wife. Since he made no attempt to quarantine his wife, it must have been the doctor himself who had the health problem he was trying to treat. Since this condition had existed for over a month, it was obviously not responding to treatment. That probably meant it was a new type of bacteria or virus that was causing the problem . . . and who at the Center was working with new strains of viruses?"

"Shoemaker was working in that area. He—"

"That's what you wanted Robinson to believe," Henry interrupted. "You had a natural villain in Professor Shoemaker, and you used him to the fullest. You convinced Robinson that Shoemaker had secretly infected him, while in fact it was you.

In your search for a virus that could be used as a sterilizing agent, you did in fact discover one. McCarthy wanted you to make your findings public. But instead you clammed up. Why?"

"You almost have it right, but not quite," Ballard sighed, slumping back in his small chair.

"Where did we go wrong?" Henry asked.

"What will you take for that tube in your pocket?"

"Sorry, it's not for sale."

"Oh, I think it is. Everyone has his price. Remember the story of the sun and the wind betting to see which could make a man take off his coat?"

"Is that a threat?"

Ballard held up his hands. "Am I in a position to threaten anyone?"

"You said we almost had it right," Becky put in. "Where did we go wrong?"

"Remember the old adage 'You can't cheat an honest man'? Well, Robinson was breaking the rules of the Center. He was testing compounds on himself. Oh, nothing dangerous; just some necessary steps in preparation for his sickle-cell detection method. But I found out what he was doing just at the same time I discovered the limits of my own sterilizing virus. Do you believe in fate, Mr. Garrott?"

"I believe in the inevitable destiny of man."

"Oh, yes. Christianity and all that. Well, I believe in *this* destiny," Ballard declared, tapping his temple with his thumb. "For just when my specialized virus was demonstrating to me just how specialized it was, along came my perfect pigeon—Robinson. My virus would disrupt the DNA chain at the pigmentation link, as I expected, but it would work only on the dark-skinned lab animals. Then, when I needed to confirm this limitation, I found Robinson falling in my lap. The guy would believe anything I told him—at first, anyway.

"I did infect him . . . through one of his own concoctions. When he developed a slight fever, I persuaded him to quarantine himself. All I had to do was sit back and observe.

"Then he noticed his skin started getting lighter. That was a side effect I wasn't planning on, but it's a logical event I should have anticipated. He finally put two-and-two together and decided it wasn't the result of anything he had done to himself. I tried everything I could think of to keep him away from the truth as long as I could. Yes, I did for a time persuade him it was Shoemaker. I even set up some dummy experiments and told him they were Shoemaker's. We supposedly would plot together to trap Shoemaker and expose him to the world.

"But then Robinson stumbled on the larger truth. He was running one of my computer programs for information about pigmentation when he pulled the wrong tape off the shelf."

"He got the addresses you had gleaned from Dr. Jones' project," Henry said.

"Yes," Ballard said with an appreciative smile. "I tried to convince him I was simply storing them for her, but I don't think he ever bought that. So then I told him I stole them from Shoemaker because he was going to use it in some way against blacks."

"Then somehow he discovered from the banker Lipert that there were funds missing," Henry continued. "He tried to get a look at the books Dr. Begelman was supposed to be keeping, and Begelman got angry over Robinson's insinuations and threw him out."

"Something like that, I suppose."

"But he'd figured out enough to know you were behind it all. And when he confronted you with this information you killed him."

"Would it mean anything to you if I told you it was an accident?" Ballard said.

"After you enticed him onto the scaffold? No. I don't think anyone would buy that."

Ballard sat dejectedly for a moment with a little-boy-forlorn look. He looked at his hands and searched for a comfortable place to put them but there was none. "Okay, okay. I'll turn myself in. I'll cooperate. I'll even say I pushed him intentionally, although that isn't true. He was the one who wanted me on the scaffold. Up until the last minute, he still thought it was Shoemaker. But when I made the mistake of showing him the correct DNA linkage for pigmentation, he put it all together in an instant. And he turned on me and started strangling the life out of me. He kept shouting, 'You're trying to kill us! You're trying to kill us!' "

"Meaning the black people."

"Of course. I had all I could do to fight him off. See here? I've still got marks on my neck."

He pushed back his collar, and there was a trace of a dark bruise visible.

"I had to push him off me with my feet. I almost lost my balance, too."

"Why didn't you stay to help him?"

"I knew you'd be there in a matter of seconds."

"So you ran down the office corridor and out the building. And the lab coat?"

"Lab coat? I don't know. I must have taken it off sometime in the building, because I didn't have it on outside."

"Then what?"

"I ran over to my car and slouched down in the back seat trying to think of what to do next. I'd worked too hard too long to have everything go down the drain now."

"Where was your car? I didn't see it in the staff lot."

"I parked on the back road. I didn't want to advertise my meeting with Robinson at that point in time."

"So you stayed in your car till you saw the ambulance and the other cars pull away and you went back into the center—"

"No," Ballard denied flatly.

"Oh?" Henry exclaimed with surprise. "Then you must have gone home to mull over your next step. You thought Robinson would live, so you had to destroy the evidence at the Center that would outline your sterilization plans. You went back to the Center that afternoon or evening, made your poor man's arson kit to destroy your own files—not the files of Robinson, as you had told me—then you packed up your wife and headed for the desert, supposedly to see the wild flowers. But the radio news broadcast in your car told you Robinson had died. Now there was no need to destroy those papers, so you raced back to town and played the part of the innocent victim—rescuing your own damaged records."

Ballard smiled. "I'd applaud if I could. Very well done. I'll admit it all. I'll even sign a confession I intentionally killed

Robinson if you'll only—"

Henry's attention was switching to the slowing city traffic ahead of them. The evening rush had come to a halt because of road construction in the next several blocks, and he was beginning to fidget.

"Is this driver taking us 'round Robin's barn?"

"Tell me—just out of curiosity," Ballard requested, "why did you suspect me and not Shoemaker?"

Henry smiled. "You were the only one of the suspects who didn't ask what I was doing at the Center. That could only mean you didn't care, or you already knew. I hardly suspected the former, especially when that night at McCarthy's you so quickly volunteered the information about the complete funding for your legitimate research work. Shoemaker, on the other hand, made a special trip into town just to find out I was an accountant.

"But the person on the Finance Committee who had been draining funds for a secret project—who had known just when certain other members were going to be out of town so they couldn't answer questions that might arise over checks forged in their name, who had sprayed water up in the attic to delay the day of reckoning when the check for the roofer's services would break the balance of the already lean bank account—that person, Professor Ballard, would be expecting a financial expert to be appearing on the scene. He didn't care about himself. He knew it was only a matter of time before he got caught. He only wanted to hold his crumbling plan together long enough to accomplish his goal of bringing the world's mushrooming population growth under control. You see, Professor, no one else had your unique interests and capabilities to put together such a plan. It had to be you, had to be you. . . . " Becky picked it up, humming a few bars from the old love song, "It Had To Be You." Father and daughter laughed nervously at their own cleverness. Ballard didn't join in.

"And maybe that motive wasn't quite as pure as you'd have us think." Henry went on, "Maybe just a trace of bitterness was left over from your son's tragic death. Just enough to turn you into a fanatic."

Ballard squirmed and turned his face away. "You make it

sound . . . it wasn't that way at all. It's a magnificent plan and it'll still work. The generations of people-to-come will praise my work."

The traffic ahead was at a standstill.

Henry fidgeted. "I wonder if the cab driver knew this street was under repair. Isn't it his business to know?"

Ballard looked at his watch, then pushed open the glass to the driver. "Take a right at the next intersection."

"Hey wait," Henry called. "Will that be the fastest way to the station?"

"It sure will," the cabbie assured, and edged over to make his right-hand turn.

"I wonder, Mr. Garrott, if you've really thought this through."

"What do you mean?"

"I mean, contrary to what Robinson shouted at me, I'm not killing anyone. The worst thing that will happen is something comparable to a light case of the flu. The gradual fading of the skin pigmentation is not altogether undesirable. It happens in many elderly blacks anyway. I'm just speeding up the process."

"And the sterilized condition?"

"I calculate that after two months of unimpaired virus activity, the condition will be irreversible. But the other side effects will diminish. The virus only has an appetite for the one amino acid."

"What about antibiotics?"

"To control it? No. It's a true virus. It'll take a vaccine to stop it."

"And there is no such vaccine, I take it."

Ballard shook his head. "I estimate that it will take three to six months before our so-called medical experts discover this is anything more than an outbreak of some flu strain. And it will take another two years before such a vaccine could be developed and produced in sufficient quantity to make any significant impact. By that time I estimate over ninety-two percent of the potential child-bearers with dominant black genes will be sterile."

"Children included?"

"Children included."

"But America is not the country with the population problem," Henry said.

"I know. Not yet, anyway. I tried to talk the advertising people into a third-world distribution scheme, but they wouldn't go for it. Besides, I only had Dr. Jones' old address file to draw from. It's no serious matter, though. The virus is very durable. I got it to thrive up to a week in a common toothpaste solution. Then it'll spread by normal social contacts. And we'll make some token mailings to the dark-skinned people of Bangladesh and East Africa. It'll be a worldwide condition in six months, and with a little benign neglect on America's part, a major catastrophe of over-population and hideous starvation will have been averted."

"And whole races, whole cultures will disappear from the earth."

"Oh, we can take pictures of their tribal dances and folksongs for the poor historians and sociologists. Besides, they'll be around for quite a few years to come. Think about it. Do we really need them? What monumental cultural contribution have they made that will be missed? Even America's basketball teams will have twenty-some years to adjust back to using white players."

Ballard smiled an innocent little smile of surprise. There was no trace of sarcasm in his statements. Just the simple twisted logic, devoid of the humor that always seems lacking in true fanatics. Henry sensed this, and rather than try to argue with the man, he decided to spend time getting more information.

"Is there anyone in this with you?"

Ballard raised himself in his seat. "No. This is all my doing. My plan entirely. Those poor simpletons at the advertising firm think I'm planning a six-million-dollar campaign on a new children's toothpaste. 'The Peabody Campaign to Stop Tooth Decay the Fun Way,' " he said melodiously. "You like that? I thought of it myself the night Bertha Corbut died."

"The day you voted against their campaign."

"Of course, of course. I couldn't very well have those two old biddies about if I was to use their mailing list and their advertising connections." Getting carried away with his story, Ballard started making a fist to gesture, but the pain made him open his hand again. Henry continued for him.

"So when the agency returned Dr. Jones' things to her at the Center, you intercepted the package long enough to run a computer copy of her addresses."

"You're tying up all the loose ends, aren't you?" Ballard said, glancing at his watch again. Then he pushed open the glass to the driver. "Better take the shortcut under the bridge."

"Okay," the cabbie said and swerved into the left lane of the darkened street.

Henry moved forward to speak to the driver, but Ballard moved his face in the way and smiled. "Don't worry. It's the fastest way."

"Why do you keep looking at the time?" Becky ventured.

"I don't know. Nervous habit I guess."

They rode in silence through the back streets of old Cleveland. The streets and the houses all bore the obvious traits of dilapidation. There were only a few people on the streets—all of them black.

Then Henry spoke. "Now it's my turn to tell a story. There once was a very famous artist. A painter of great renown. He was recognized the world over for his craftsmanship and insight, for he was not only a great innovator but also a classisist. Then one day, after laboring over a new and innovative type art, he presented his finished product to the world. 'See what I have made!' he announced proudly. But the world was shocked at what he presented. They turned away in disgust, laughing and ridiculing the artist. And the artist went away sorrowing."

Ballard scowled and shook his head slowly. "You can save your efforts, my friend. Your story is built on a faulty premise. For you see, there is no artist behind the universe. No painter. No creator. The only creator in all the world is the mind of man freed from the baloney of irrational faiths."

"Ah, but it is you, my friend, who has the irrational faith, for you believe that nobody, plus nothing, equals everything. That's quite a formula to hang your life on. I'd like to have you explain it to me some time, because it seems to require a good deal more blind faith than I can muster."

Ballard's face went blank. He looked again at his watch and stared passively out the window. Henry persisted.

"I don't know why there is suffering in the world—why people die of malnutrition. But I do know it isn't the will of God. I don't know about Shoemaker's theory—about blacks being intellectually inferior to others. It really isn't my concern. What I do know is that they are children of God. He made them, He cares for them, and Christ died for their sins just like He died for mine. Can't you see that? He wants only good for them—for all of us. He gave us the whole world to enjoy and use, and He showed us how to treat each other—with love and compassion."

Ballard kept gazing out the window, showing no sign of response.

"And to top it all off, He gave us the hope of the Resurrection—to be with Him in a paradise beyond our wildest dreams. Can you imagine that? Think of your two sons whole and happy. Not with their frail earthly bodies, poor lungs, and crumpled bones, but perfect—"

Ballard burst out with a sob and dropped his head down on his arms, swaying from side to side. "I'd give anything, anything to believe that."

"You can believe it," Henry encouraged, "because it's all true. You can bank on it because of Christ. Isn't that wonderful?"

Ballard slowly raised his head. His eyes were red and wet. He looked out the window for a moment, then said, "We better stop by those phones."

"What for?" Henry asked.

"Part of a shipment is scheduled to leave the post office at nine o'clock. We won't get there in time to stop it."

Henry leaned forward to the driver. "Pull over by those phones up ahead." He looked at Ballard. "Who do we call? The post office isn't going to interrupt mail deliveries on just a phone call."

The cab pulled over next to the bank of three outdoor phones and stopped.

"Ask for the night supervisor. He can put a twenty-four

hour delay on any substance that is produced to be ingested," Ballard offered. "You want me to call? But I—"

"Never mind. I'll call," Henry grunted, hopping out of the cab and fumbling for change. "What post office?"

"The Terminal Annex."

Henry finally found the right change, hurried across the grubby sidewalk and tried the phone. The first one wouldn't accept his money. He moved on to the next. He put in the necessary money and waited—but nothing was happening.

"Here, Daddy."

Henry turned to see Becky extending a slip of paper to him.

"Oh, honey, wait in the cab, okay?"

Suddenly the cab door slammed shut. The engine revved and the vehicle sped away from the curb and up the street. Ballard was crouched up close to the driver, apparently talking to him to distract his attention from Henry's frantic waves. Henry chased them to the corner and half way into the intersection before giving up. After watching them drive out of sight, Henry came back to the phones and tried the third one. It was out of order also, the cash box having been torn out.

"Oh, Daddy, I'm sorry," Becky lamented. "I thought he was ready to help us."

Henry took the note from Becky's hand and unfolded it. "What does it say?"

"See how you like your painting now," Henry read slowly.

He went around the corner to check for any stores that might be open. It was a small neighborhood complex of three shops. All were closed—the liquor store seemed to be out of business, and the grocery store and drugstore were closed for the night. Steel accordion fencing had been pulled across the front of all three, and they were locked tight. The store front windows bore the telltale markings of no-nonsense burglar alarms.

"It appears we've been dropped into the heart of one of the city's toughest black ghettos."

"He told me he was writing a phone number," Becky tried to explain.

"Yes, never mind."

For a few minutes they stood at the lighted street corner,

looking up and down the silent streets, pondering their next move. Henry wondered why Ballard had known so much about Cleveland, if he had known the phones were out of commission, or if he'd just assumed from former experiences. None of this was verbalized. The thing to do now was to get himself and his daughter into the hands of the police.

While they were still plotting their next action, a group of young blacks ambled into the light from somewhere behind the stores. Their lighthearted chatter stopped when they saw the two whites standing under the lights. Slowly and silently, they drifted past, then looked back.

"Boys, can you tell me where we can get to a phone?" Henry tried to sound friendly. "All these seem to be out of order."

They looked at one another; an older fellow, sporting a grey, broad-brimmed fedora, stepped forward. "Yeah, man, you can use my aunt's phone."

"Where might that be?"

"Right there," the fedora tilted. "Second house."

"Okay, let's go," Henry ordered, and the group moved toward the second house. As they approached the front walk of the old two-story frame house, Henry felt the restraint of a hand on his shoulder.

"Tell me, mister. How come you call us 'boy'," the fedora spat. Several other voices chimed in with their own complaints, and the circle around Henry and Becky tightened.

"Look, can I make the phone call or not?"

"How much you willin' to pay for it?"

Before Henry could reach his wallet, several other hands helped themselves. He tried to resist, but found himself being forced, face down, into the weeds of the front yard. Becky had been trying to hold onto him but her arm was ripped away. As his face was pushed harder into the ground, he felt several hands nimbly running through his pockets. Becky screamed for help, but her cries were muffled as the fedora barked out instructions to keep the noise down.

After Henry's pockets had been stripped and his watch yanked from his wrist, he found the gang's attention shifting from himself to Becky. With only two of the young blacks holding him down, he rolled over onto his side in time to see Becky being forced into the bushes in the front of the house.

His adrenalin surging, he broke away from his two captors, who immediately snapped into judo stances in front of the bushes. Instead of fighting them, Henry whirled and ran for the lighted street corner. Once there, he clambered hand-over-hand up the front of the grocery store's steel fence, then squeezed his left foot through the bars against the middle of the glass window. With a quick jab, the glass shattered and the jangling of the burglar alarm pierced the heavy night air.

He performed the same stunt on the large drugstore window, setting off another alarm in a nerve-grating duet.

Reaching into the display window, Henry snatched a small electric razor in its case and a long dagger of the broken glass. Jamming the blunt edge of the glass against the heel of his bandaged left hand, he raced back down the street toward Becky.

Passing the first house, he lobbed the razor through the lighted front window. Two deep-voiced dogs began barking.

Approaching the bushes, he found no need for his makeshift weapon as the noise of the alarms and Becky's screams were waking the neighborhood. Lights appeared in windows, and the last of the young tough guys scampered through a yard and out of sight. Becky was sobbing and running her hands around in the dry leaves in search of her shoe.

"Are you all right, honey?"

She grabbed her shoe and rushed into her father's arms. By the time the police arrived, nearly thirty people had gathered around the frightened white couple. Most were just rubbernecking, but a few stepped forward with offers of help and sympathy.

At the local police station, Henry refused to cooperate with the officers until he was granted the use of the telephone. At approximately ten-fifteen, he got his hands on a phone on a desk sergeant's desk. He dialed the special 800 number his old bureau had given him. After many clicks and nervous pauses, he was connected.

"Hello."

"This is an emergency," Henry said. "Let me speak with U. S. Twilligar, please."

"One moment," the voice said and more clicks and buzzes ensued.

The desk sergeant watched Henry suspiciously. Becky reached over and put her hand over the mouthpiece of the phone.

"What are you going to say?"

"I'm going to tell them everything."

"About the toothpaste?"

"Yes."

Becky studied her father's eyes for a moment. "But if you don't—"

"We'd be playing right into Ballard's hands. We've got to."

Becky sat back in her chair, with the police officer's eyes flitting back and forth between the two of them.

Finally a voice identifying itself as U. S. Twilligar came on the line, and Henry proceeded to explain about the ominous toothpaste about to be delivered. He intentionally left out the details of the virus involving only blacks, just in case Ballard's theory of benign neglect was about to be implemented early.

Henry was surprised to see how much influence and respect his old bureau still commanded despite its recent bad publicity. The police stopped talking about pressing charges for destruction of property. Instead they served coffee and doughnuts, which Becky and Henry found exceptionally tasty, and within an hour of the phone call, the Chief of Police arrived to shake their hands very graciously.

The entire shipment, he informed them, was still in the post office—none had been shipped early as Ballard had indicated. They were taking steps to isolate all the workers who had been at the Effervescent plant, and extensive tests were already being run on the paste to determine its exact danger to the community.

Henry gave them a detailed description of Ballard and all information about the Kilbourne Center. The Chief wanted to call a press conference in order to make the early morning papers. He wanted Henry with him, but Henry declined—even having his picture taken—claiming his continued need for secrecy as an excuse.

They were finally driven to their motel around one-thirty, Cleveland time.

It wasn't until Henry's head had hit the pillow, and he tried to pray, that he realized the irony of what he had done that day. He slid his feet out the side of the bed and sat up, holding his head in his hands, perhaps thinking that somehow the upright position was better for giving and receiving a lecture.

You hypocrite! What are you doing? You diddle away your career job and allow yourself to be dismissed because of your new moral stance—The Agency is bad, but I can be good. And the first time out, under pressure, you lie, steal, you stand ready to kill. And worst of all, you feel no remorse about it at all! You'd do it all over again. Can you justify that? Is there a solid piece of ground you can stand on?

"O Lord, when do I hit the wall? When do I know what actions a Christian should take? Is it meekly back to the lions, or what? You know I want to be your man. I want to do justly, to love mercy, and walk humbly with you. But it's hard. With all the willing spirit in the world, I still need your grace.

"I guess the ball is in your court, because I can't think of anything more to say. Except, my back is killing me. Good night."

Thursday

"Henry, we have guests," Valery called from the dining room window.

Valery's call found him in the garden trying to get Mrs. Begelman's succulent clippings started. It was so much easier to work in the garden since they had hired a professional gardener. Somehow he knew the necessary things would be done whether or not he did them and the acts that before seemed a drudgery now were genuinely fun. He wondered about the psychology of all that as he got to his feet, brushed off his hands against his sweatshirt, and headed inside. At the doorway, he stopped and dutifully slipped out of his dirty loafers.

In the living room Valery was standing with Wilma Robinson and an older black woman Henry took to be her mother. When she saw her husband she gasped and pointed at his feet.

"Oh, Henry, you have no shoes on," he mimicked.

The ladies laughed at Henry's joke, while Valery hurried into the bedroom to find something for his feet. Wilma introduced her mother, Mrs. Brown, and the three sat down, Henry taking the only living room chair Valery allowed him to sit in when he was in his work clothes.

Mrs. Brown explained that they were on their way to the airport but wanted to stop by and thank Henry for his part in "the Dr. Robinson matter."

"You'll be happy to know," she announced, "that our junior Senator from Illinois will be introducing legislation to curb the activities of scientists who experiment with dangerous viruses, and the like."

"Oh, I didn't know about that," Henry said.

"Yes, my husband called me last night, giving me the news. That should make you very proud."

"Oh. Yes, well, I guess I'm not very impressed with laws written by men."

Mrs. Brown and her daughter exchanged inquisitive glances; then Wilma asked, "Has there been any word about Professor Ballard yet?"

"Yes, I'm afraid there has. Last night I received a call from the Ohio State Police asking for his description. Apparently he was involved in a one-car accident and managed to kill himself."

"Oh, how awful! You think he committed suicide?"

"That would be my guess," Henry said; "although we can't say for sure. I suppose he made it look accidental for insurance purposes. How is his wife getting along, do you know?"

"We tried to see her before we left. She had a healthy baby girl, you know."

"No, I didn't know."

"Yes. She's getting along fine," Wilma said, playing with the strap on her traveling purse. "They were hoping for a girl you know, so's it wouldn't remind them of . . . "

Her lip started quivering, and her mother ran her hand along the crest of her shoulders.

"I'm so sorry for her," Wilma said softly. "They was such good friends, you know. I just can't understand why he'd do such a thing. Do you think he pushed Greg off intentionally?"

"He told me it was an accident . . . although he was awfully good at lying. I think it's one of those things we'll never know. It's hard to know, sometimes, why people do the things they do, especially if something shakes the whole foundation of their lives and they don't have a strong faith they can fall back on. I thought for a while that he might have been the victim of a split personality. Perhaps something like that did happen.

"Are you going back to Chicago?" he questioned.

"Yes."

"Good. I think that's a splendid idea. Get a new start and all."

"Mr. Garrott, why do you suppose Greg wrote that letter to the post office people?"

"I'm not sure. Either he'd found out about the addresses that someone was going to use for illegal mailings, or what seems more logical, he was trying to report the illegal opening of Dr. Jones' package. He was definitely on the right track, and if it hadn't been for his work, we probably would never have gotten onto Ballard.

"But I think the thing for you to concentrate on, young lady, is that your husband loved you after all, and he was trying to do the right thing for you."

"That's just what I keep telling her," Mrs. Brown declared.

"I know, I know. I jus' wish he'd confided in me, that's all," Wilma said, then blinked through her tears and managed a smile.

Later that morning, the front door slammed with a startling thud.

"Man, does he have nerve!" Becky sputtered, standing in the doorway leading out onto the patio. She had been doing some morning shopping, and now came over to the patio table and plopped down. Henry and Valery had just finished a leisurely brunch and were sharing sections of the morning paper.

"What's your problem, young lady?" Valery demanded.

"Where's the front section? Here, turn to page three. Did you read that?"

"The McCarthy thing?" Henry replied with a smirk. "Yes, I did."

"Of all the nerve. You'd think he did the whole thing single-handedly. Listen to this: 'I was brought on staff here because of my troubleshooting record with the State Department, and it wasn't long before I had spotted the problem with Ballard's project. We wanted suspicion to be thrown onto Shoemaker so that Ballard would be free to play his hand, and we could catch him redhanded. It was all cut and dried then. Just a matter of having my agents spring the trap.' "

Henry laughed. "What did you expect him to say?"

" 'My agents,' indeed! Why, the whole thing's a pack of lies. He didn't know what was going on."

"Hindsight is wonderful, isn't it?"

"Why does he say things like that anyway?"

"For the same reason Vernon McCarthy does everything he does. To advance or strengthen his own position in life. That's why I was hired in the first place, and that's why he fired me. And I'm sure that was his reason for putting Ballard's lab coat in Shoemaker's file drawer."

"He did? McCarthy did that?"

"When I saw him in the hospital Saturday afternoon, his mind was going sixty miles an hour when I suggested Shoemaker's guilt would be good for the Center. He no doubt saw the lab coat thrown in some corner, probably in the hallway of the office wing; he wanted the case wrapped up quickly for the sake of public relations and figured helping the case along with a little extra evidence wouldn't hurt."

"How can you be so sure of that?"

"Oh, it's rather obvious. Doesn't it seem just a bit odd that the police would start searching his effects so quickly? They'd only brought charges against him Saturday evening. I have a feeling McCarthy unlocked Shoemaker's office door for them, and made sure his file drawers were gone over. And remember, the only ones with master keys to all the locks were Miss

Matthews and Vern McCarthy."

"Why that, that . . . he's just as bad as Ballard!"

Henry laughed. "What do you propose we do about it?"

"Why, he can be arrested for planting evidence. That's illegal."

"I don't think we could get it to stick."

"Well, at least we should report him to the Board of the Kilbourne Foundation," Becky fumed.

"Maybe so, but he'd probably talk his way out of it. I *was* his agent, you know, and I *did* solve his problem, as he said. How can we prove he didn't know Ballard was guilty? And the only one who could bring charges against him would be Shoemaker in a civil suit, which I doubt he's willing to do."

Becky slumped back in her chair and pouted.

"Don't feel too bad, honey. I have a feeling McCarthy will have to do all the scratching and clawing he can just to keep that place going after this fiasco. He said himself that think-tanks have little more than reputations to go on. Unless they can come up with something new and startling in the area of research, I think their days are numbered."

"Well, I hope so."

While they were talking, Valery had gone into the living room to answer the phone; she came back out with a twinkle in her eye.

"Henry, you'll never guess who that is on the phone."

"Who?"

"It's your old agency boss."

"Chapin? You're kidding!"

Valery quickly shook her head, then nodded.

"Calling for *me*?"

"He wants you to look into a matter for him down San Diego way."

"Well, what do you think of that?" He turned to Becky. "He's the one who ordered me into the detention ward. Well, well."

"Henry," Valery scolded.

"If I go down there for him, I wonder if he'll give me time off for Bible study."

"Oh, Henry, will you stop trying to be funny and go talk to the man?"